Portrait of Little Boy in Darkness

Daniel McGuire

TEAL PRESS

Portsmouth, New Hampshire

Book design by R.D. Jebb
Cover painting: "Portrait of Little Boy" by Juan Carlos Blanca

First Edition October 1986
Printed in the United States of America

Published by Teal Press, P.O. Box 4346, Portsmouth,
New Hampshire 03801

Library of Congress Cataloging-in-Publication Data

McGuire, Daniel, 1936-
    Portrait of Little Boy in darkness.

    I. Title.
PS3563.C3682P6 1986   813'.54   86-50144
ISBN 0-913793-04-3

Epilogue 1

A huge brick room in a huge brick building. This is Little Boy's home. The walls of this room tower high above the rest of the building to a steep-sloped roof. The roof is comprised of stained-glass panels that form a beautiful skylight. The room is empty, as is the entire building.

Little Boy is outside, standing at the edge of a small park. He is trying to get back inside his room but has forgotten the way. There are several paths but he doesn't know which one leads to the door. He can see parts of the building, but most of it is obscured by trees and bushes.

Obituary

Jonathan is dead. He is buried, a perpetual light burning over his grave, deep in the gray matter of my brain. His coffin is open and light shines down on his still form. His blue eyes are closed in eternal sleep. Though the light is always there, I see him through a darkening haze. I want to reach out and touch him but I am afraid he is cold. I want to sweep the darkness away but it is there for a reason.

I love Jonathan, just as I love all dead children, but I wish he wasn't dead. I wish he could open his eyes and see me and tell me that he loves me as much as I love him.

Dim shadows make his face look sad and hopelessly frozen; they pull him farther and farther away from me. He knows I can no longer touch him, and I fear he hates me because of this. He cannot hear me when I say I'm sorry for not being what he wanted me to be.

I wish myself dead and cold with him.

All I want is one chance to make the past solid, but it is elusive and fragmented, obscured by the dust of time until the real melds with the magic. The faces of all children become the face of Jonathan, and his face

2

becomes the face of all children, sinking with their bodies into the crude interiors of tiny coffins. Eyes, once burning with life, are closed in unknowing sleep and will not open to my pleas. I whisper in their ears but they are beyond hearing. My tears fall upon their cheeks and that is the only contact possible. Still, they cannot feel the wetness, nor can their mouths form the words that all is well with them, that I must forget, for they are only dead children who cannot understand, can no longer feel sorrow.

The faces decay, the eyes rot in their sockets, the skin becomes wrinkled, the hair turns white, the lips become thin and cracked. Even Jonathan's face appears old and dark with knowledge.

But now, in the stillness, I see that one of the bodies is breathing though still collapsed in death, and as I back off in revulsion, I realize that the body is my own.

Only now are the ravages clear and obvious. Jonathan died of a cancer that devoured him so slowly he had been unaware of his declining health or the changes that had taken place within him. He was aware of only the symptoms: the questions that went unanswered, the questions that were met with rage, the questions he became afraid to ask. He died alone, uncomforted by loved ones. He was not even aware of his own demise.

There are no survivors; all were obliterated with his passing.

Services drag on forever.

Picture From an Album

Late spring sunlight slanting down the bank. It catches the top of the wide wooden chair, glances off Sis's hair and Baby's forehead, then splashes against Joe's broad back. More sunlight touches the top of Teddy's head as he sits beside Sis, lunchbox nestled in his lap. Willie's back is to the camera. He is more concerned about helping Joe hold the other lunchbox. Sunlight brightens his hair and the light-colored suit he wears appears darker because of this. The rest of the sunlight strikes the side of the stairs leading from the road to the flat stretch of ground at basement level and against the house itself. The overgrown bank and rocky terrace are in shadow.

Sis sits wedged into the corner where the chair's arm meets the backrest. Her feet extend a couple of inches beyond the front of the seat, angled toward the camera. Baby sits on her lap as though she was a chair herself. The back of his head presses lightly against her turned cheek, and his body follows her contour until it gives out somewhere short of her ankles. He is dressed in a warm sweater with a blanket covering his lower half.

Teddy is not trusting the camera. His gaze goes out timidly to meet the lens as though it was a seedy old man clutching a bag of bad tricks. His left hand is raised close to his chin, its fingers curled loosely over the top of a schoolbook but poised to reach up in self-defense, or to be stuck in his uncertain mouth.

Sis's face is blank. It merely says: I am here. Her left hand has slid under Baby's left armpit and, with maternal tenderness, is placed protectively over his heart. Her right arm is under his outstretched right arm but that hand is at the side of his head. Only the fingers touch. They gently direct his face to the camera. The pinky is separated from the other fingers, catching the corner of his eye to set up an intimate and direct line of communication.

Willie's expression is hidden. Only the recess of his eye can be seen, and the roundness of his cheek, but there is an impression of good humor.

Joe sits on the end of the armrest, his back a few inches from Baby's hand. Like Teddy, he wears a sweater, dark pants, and new shoes. His left hand reaches down. It is together with Willie's hand on the lunchbox handle, but his attention is focused on the camera. His right hand clutches schoolbooks to his chest but he is unaware of them. There is only a hint of timidity on his face. His eyes are confident and more outgoing than the others. His smile is mischievous, coming easily but at the same time reluctant to the point of half-understood obligation and formality.

Baby is not exactly bewildered. His eyes are wide-open with curiosity while a question is about to bubble from his mouth. He doesn't realize that it will come out sounding silly, but perhaps he holds it back anyway. His gaze is centered on the camera lens. Mostly, he is aware of Sis's hands, the strength of her soft and bony body, and he is content to just sit there. It does not occur to him, nor would it seem important if it did, that there is more to life than this.

Sickness

Lying in bed, shivering and fevered, he groans at the turmoil that has infiltrated his body. The stagnant air is oppressive; the world feels distant. He has been forgotten and is allowed to sink slowly into the darkness of oblivion. At times, he rolls over to the edge of the bed to spew yellow vomit into the chamber pot, then rests there awhile because his head is too heavy to move, eyes moist from the exertion and from the pungent odor of the pot's mixed contents, lips and mouth tasting of bile.

Some days, even when he is up and about, weakness leaves him unable to walk and transporting him becomes Sis's responsibility. This barely registers on his consciousness, not at all on his memory, but he knows, without having to think about it, that she does so without complaint or expectations of any reward. If he does give it any thought, it is only to the degree of sensing a similarity between her and Mother and of being warmed by the comparison. Yet he feels the chilly difference and distance between the female and male members of the family and wonders with fright at what is expected of him, if they will come to demand that he choose sides and become either one or the other. These thoughts only serve to draw the sickness deeper into his body until the fever sears the nerves that connect him to the life force and threatens to burn him completely away.

It is during one of these gallbladder attacks, on a night they think they might lose him, that Jonathan experiences one of the most pleasant moments of his life. The other children have been sent off to their beds; he has been allowed to stay up with Mother and Father, a treat that has never been granted him before. The three of them are in the dining room, Father sitting at the end of the table, Mother at the side, and Jonathan lies stretched out across two chairs between them. He is partly beneath the table so that it forms a barrier, along with the wall behind him, against the night, his head near Father's knee and his feet pressed securely into Mother's side.

The kerosene lamp sends its faint light into the room, leaving the corners in threatening dimness and throwing slow-moving shadows across the wall, but he senses no danger in them. Mother and Father speak softly to each other. He knows they are not talking about him, but that doesn't matter; it is enough that they keep their voices low and gentle for his sake. This and a number of other things make him sleepy, but he fights to stay awake; he wants this night to last forever, these voices to continue talking and never stop, this feeling of closeness to those who protect him to never end. But, as his resolve weakens and the conscious resistance to sinking gradually fades, the darkness floats in as more of a friend than he has ever thought possible, and he lets it carry him off in much the same way Father sometimes carries him to bed.

With Mother

In the dark kitchen, she is scrubbing the morning dishes. Her body is round like a ball; her heavy hands swish a shiny pot about in the water. She is part of the darkness, much like those Gypsy women who steal babies, but her darkness is that of silent patience and ages upon ages of mysterious knowledge. Her eyes follow with genuine interest the swirling motion of her hand, but they ignore Jonathan as he watches from the doorway. As her thick arms move together, he notices two bulges of fat upon her chest, is distracted momentarily, then returns to admiring her face.

Suddenly, a spot of light dances upon the ceiling. It moves back and forth from wall to wall, above his head then into the corner, fading momentarily only to return across the way. He wishes that Mother would look up and notice this strange object, but her attention remains fixed on her work.

"What's that?" he finally asks, pointing a finger.

She does not move her head but acts as though she has seen the light all along. "That's the Easter Bunny."

Words fail Jonathan. Head tilted back, he stares upward, awed by Mother's sly wisdom and the Bunny's

8

clever disguise.

"He's watching you to make sure you're good."

In the evening, he is once more alone with her in the kitchen. The darkness is deeper now, the lamp's dim light casting heavy shadows about her and through the room. Harder and harder he stares at her calm face but she doesn't seem to know that he is there. On tiptoes, he reaches up to scrub his hands in the basin's warm water, again and again squeezing the soap, then rubbing it into his flesh, each time removing another layer of dirt, hoping she will notice how pure he is making himself.

Another day finds them on the porch together in bright sunlight, gazing uproad at the papermill. A large black car crosses the bridge to their side of the creek, then turns southward toward the house.

Mother moves with surprising speed. She hurries Jonathan inside, closes and locks the door all in one motion, then guides him into the living room. "Don't make a sound," she whispers as she closes the curtains. She returns to him, placing her hands on his shoulders to gently encourage his obedience.

He likes this; knows he will not displease her; suffers the question itching in his mind and silently vows to defend Mother with all his might against whatever evil is about to threaten her. Only moments pass before a rapping comes at the door. She rocks Jonathan, loving him more than ever in their conspiracy.

After the rapping ceases, she breathes loudly, then, without so much as a rewarding kiss, urges him on ahead of her down the stairs to the kitchen.

With Father

"I can run across the road before that car gets here," Jonathan tells Willie, referring to a black Ford chugging around the nearby bend. He has already leaped from the porch and is onto the macadam before Willie replies, "Bet you can't."

Jonathan feels he is a blur of movement, like the wind, that there is magic in his legs. He dives for the ditch just as a huge shape looms black and threatening and a screech of brakes jolts his senses. He rolls over into a sitting position and stares up at the horrified driver's face, trying to explain with his eyes, that there had been no need for such dramatics, that he, Jonathan, had been in no danger, but the man turns his head away to shout through the open side window.

"He could have been killed!"

Jonathan cranes his neck so he can see down the stairs at the side of the house. Father is in the doorway, nodding his head in agreement with something the man in the car is saying. The conversation is brief but Jonathan does not catch it; he is thinking that poor judgment has been used and he is not sure it was his. After all, he did prove his point to Willie and that should mean something.

The car moves on but Father remains in the doorway, his hand reaching out with its finger beckoning.

Jonathan stands poised with his hand on the doorknob as inner forces pull him in opposite directions. Fear insists that he open the door: In his mind, he sees his brothers running, screaming, down the steep bank toward the creek, then back up again, Father hobbling after them, belt in hand, the inevitable punishment meted out with more vigor than usual because of their attempted escape. Jonathan sees himself fleeing down the road, Father in close pursuit. He tries to gauge his chances for success while grasping desperately for some solid chunk of courage, but it seems to be melting away like ice in fire.

He watches the belt slip slowly from one loop after another, feels himself suffocating in the dark pools of unforgiving fury which are Father's eyes, wishes that this most powerful of men had just a little softness so he could feel the terror now beating wildly in his son's chest. Jonathan tells himself he will not be like his brothers; he will be brave, but as the belt slips through the final loop, his hand turns the knob, though even he knows it is too late and a futile gesture in any case, and he feels Father's hand grasp his arm in a firm grip. For a moment, a look of amusement obliterates the stern countenance, but the face quickly reverts to its old ways.

Jonathan knows, now, that Father had been testing him, and he has failed the test.

The Bogeyman

One sunny morning, while playing behind the house, Jonathan came to realize that he was alone. The other children were at school and Mother was in the kitchen. Looking around, he sought to determine if any danger might be present, and, indeed, something sinister appeared to be in the neighborhood; beyond the corner of the building, perhaps, tiptoeing down the narrow strip of bank between the wall and the family dump; or beyond the toolshed at the opposite end of the terrace, hiding in the weeds surrounding the well in that nook where Father's property came to a point and ended at the side of a rocky cliff, where the road curved away and a tottering old ghost house leaned out over the precipice, always on the verge of collapsing onto the rapids far below.

His eyes caught a movement somewhere down the bank amid thickets and trees; a shadow that flowed into other shadows, animate into inanimate, coldly but hungrily eyeing him from a distance, trying to entice him with gentle murmurs to come to it. Instead, he wisely turned away and hurried into the house.

At night, he and Willie are often punished for talking in bed or some other malefaction, being made by Mother to lie with their arms outside the blankets. During these times, strange creatures visit them in the darkness, soundlessly threatening to grab them by their exposed limbs and carry them to a land of unimaginable evil. Zombies lurk, almost invisible, in every corner; peculiar noises issue from beneath the bed; eerie movements are sensed and sometimes seen; snakes slither along the blanket beside their bodies while wolves with fiery eyes and steamy breaths settle on their chests, crushing them until they cannot breathe or cry out for help, drooling hot juices onto their tender faces, putting them through unbearable torture until, after endless hours, they finally fall asleep.

There is one being that is always present and overseeing the harm that threatens Jonathan. It is the bogeyman, that fearsome shadow incessantly lurking in the corners of one's eyes; he who steals little boys and girls and carries them away to his foul home where he can have his wicked pleasure with them; he who is too cowardly to enter children's homes but waits for them to come outside, alone, where they will be helpless in his power.

One night, Jonathan saw the bogeyman hiding in the woods near his uncle's house. Cousin Darlene had seen him first and had pointed him out to the others, though, after thinking it over, she said she really wasn't sure. There was no moon in the sky, and the faint light coming from a nearby window did little to increase visibility.

While the other children were discussing this, Jonathan peered through the darkness with all his might. Something moved in a grove of trees, a man in a black hat that was pulled down almost to the turned-up collar of his coat. His face was black, too. At first, Jonathan thought he could see through the bogeyman, then that he was looking inside of him. The blackness was so deep and evil that it frightened him, yet he felt safe because Joe and Teddy were there. He couldn't see the bogey-

13

man's eyes but could feel them watching him. He wondered what would happen to him if the others weren't
there but was afraid to ask.

Flying

In his dream, Jonathan is standing atop a smoke-
stack inside the papermill. Far below, people gaze up at
him with wide-open mouths. The roof curves up toward
him but is obscure at this point. He can see the creek
and the waterfall and, on the other side of the road, a
wooded hill and the huge brick house where Father's
boss lives. Jonathan spreads his arms, pushes off into the
surrounding dimness, then glides slowly downward, surprising everyone with his skill and grace.

Sis

Her bedroom is on the top floor. It is off-limits to her brothers but Jonathan is occasionally taken there to play house. He is not, however, allowed to be a father; his part in the game is that of a son who is sometimes directed to hold one of the dolls to keep it from crying.

Sis is the recipient of more paternal directives than any other member of the family, it being deemed most important that she grow up to be a respectable lady. Father frequently reminds her: "Keep your legs together when you're sitting"; "Nice girls don't do that." She is taught to set the table, sweep floors, and take care of little brother. In turn, lessons on morality and proper behavior are passed on to him.

Unlike Joe and Teddy, she attends Sunday school regularly and has been smitten by a fanatical love for God. At home, she stresses the importance to Jonathan of Loving Him and His Son Jesus, of being good so that when he dies, he might be taken to Heaven to live with Them and the angels.

On one overcast day, she points to a ray of sunlight piercing the clouds and knowingly informs Jonathan, "There's Heaven. That's where God lives."

Jonathan is impressed. Where the light shines through, the clouds are bright and silvery. He estimates the spot to be exactly above the highest point of the hill across the street, about halfway between their house and the papermill. He crouches for a better view, following the light beam up through the hole in the clouds hoping for a glimpse of God, or at least an angel, but he sees nothing more than clouds and light.

Sometime in the near future, he will try to find the spot again, searching the now clear-blue sky above the hilltop for a tunnel of light and perhaps a patch of silver. But the sky is uniform everywhere, with nothing to indicate where Heaven had been. He would like to ask Sis to point it out again, but she is not present at the time. When she does become available, he will have forgotten to ask.

Epilogue 2

It is nighttime and Little Boy is sitting at the bottom of a dark, enclosed stairwell. There is just enough light to allow him to see the other children. With the exception of one girl, they are younger than he. They are pulling down each other's short pants, then giggling. There is little sexual meaning to their play, the act being done mostly to inconvenience, but it is obvious that their tutor had ulterior motives. Little Boy watches the girl pull down the pants of a little boy, making him laugh, then pull them up again.

She is sitting next to Little Boy but suddenly stands. She is about six years old, has dark hair, dark mysterious eyes, and a pretty but serious face. She turns her back to him, facing the nearby door, then leans forward to peek through the keyhole. On an impulse, Little Boy tugs gently at her slacks. She does not react and he wonders if she would get mad if he did pull them down. He is afraid because she is older and stronger. But he gathers all his courage, tugs again but harder, and the slacks come down. He stares at her round bottom and feels a certain naughtiness, a growing darkness taking hold of the girl's spirit and his own. Still, he studies her

18

with an artist's critical eye. He thinks she has a beautiful bottom. It isn't skinny, sickly white, or bony. It seems to be well-scrubbed and doesn't stink, so it isn't even nasty, which strikes him as being odd.

After several seconds, the girl turns, hands on hips, feigning anger, and Little Boy finds himself staring at her lower belly. He sees a cleft between the girl's legs and wonders at this. The flesh here is also dark, and he follows it around her side, back to what is still visible of her bottom. It is all smooth and he senses warmth beneath the surface. A nice feeling comes over him. He is grateful to the girl for letting him see her private parts. He knows she has done this because she likes him. He thinks there is something missing, though, and wishes he knew what it was.

As Little Boy sits staring at the soft, warm skin, he feels her eyes staring down at his face. They seem to be tugging at him, imploring him to look up, but he is afraid to. There is tension in those eyes. He is sure it is part of that mysterious darkness and that it is trying to capture his soul.

An Introduction to Death

One day, a car stopped in front of the house. Aunt Jane sat behind the steering wheel and Uncle Bob on the passenger side. Mother was standing on the porch. "I'm taking Bob to the hospital," Aunt Jane said.

Uncle Bob gazed straight ahead through the windshield. Jonathan hoped the man would look at him and smile, but the head didn't move.

Mother nodded and the car pulled away with nothing further being said.

Sometime later, Jonathan found Mother sobbing against the Kalamazoo stove. When he asked what was wrong, she said, "Uncle Bob is dead."

He wondered what it meant to be dead. Lady, their big black dog, had grown old and blind and had been put to sleep by Father, but that had happened far away and had never been explained to him. He knew only that death was something so terrible that it made Mother cry. To show his sympathy and hide his ignorance, he also cried.

But understanding could not be kept from him forever. It came on a sunny day as he stood alone on the porch. Gypper, their new dog, had gone across the road

20

on some adventure and was just returning to the house when a tractor-trailer came around the bend on its way to the mill. Jonathan heard the screech of brakes and looked up in time to see Gypper go under the front wheel. The truck came to a halt but the dog had already been crushed, a puddle of blood forming rapidly around him.

Jonathan screamed. Something surged through his chest, like a heart exploding with unsensed pain. "Mommy! Mommy! Mommy!" He called for her again and again even after she had rushed through the doorway out into the road to calmly scoop the animal's remains into a cardboard box. Finally, he fell silent, watching through tear-filled eyes as Mother kindly accepted the driver's apology.

It was the end of Gypper, he realized. The dog would never be alive again. At last, he thought, he knew what death meant, and he was not pleased.

The Whistler

Sometimes a man walked by the house, whistling as he went, and this intrigued Jonathan. One day, hearing the man approach, he crept up the bank to the roadside to see this happy wonder. The first thing he perceived was the gray of the man's workpants, then the long springy strides of his legs.

The man stopped directly in front of Jonathan, who gazed up at the unfamiliar face surprised that he had been noticed. He saw a hand reach into a pocket, come back out, then reach down to him. He held out his own hand and a penny fell into it. The man winked at him, then continued on his way, still whistling.

Jonathan was overwhelmed by his good fortune. He wondered what he could buy with the money. A pleasant warmth swept through him as he watched the nice man turn the bend and disappear from sight.

At the Movies

"You'd better watch out," Joe says. "Those are real bullets they're using."

"Can they come out here?" Jonathan asks.

Joe nods grimly but shows no fear. He has already informed his little brother that the cowboys and horses are real; they are actually there behind the screen upon which, by some obscure process, their images are thrown.

Jonathan slides down in his seat, hoping that any stray bullets will fly harmlessly over his head. He wonders how Joe and the others, all those surrounding him in the parquet of the theatre, in fact, can be so calm considering the circumstances. Mother, her bulk conveniently nestled to his left, has made no protective movement toward him, as though she has not heard Joe's warning.

Light flickers above his head and flashes onto the screen, enabling the audience to see the action. He slides farther down, feeling somewhat safe behind the person seated before him, occasionally peeking around that head and through the dark sea of silent bodies at the bloodshed and mayhem that spellbinds Joe, Teddy, Willie, and Sis; even Mother and Father. A bullet could

23

strike him at any instant, he realizes, and no one would ever know. He would lie bleeding to death in the darkness of the theater, unable to move or cry out, and they would go away without him and would never know his fate; they would not even remember he had ever existed and so would never come back for him. He wonders if others have already been shot and are merely corpses sitting in their seats, nobody aware of, or caring about, what has happened to them.

A sense of relief floods through him when the shooting finally stops. He pulls himself back up to his former position, wondering if anyone has noticed his cowardice.

On the screen, Cotton leaps onto the train to sit beside his girlfriend, having made a split-second but momentous decision to leave with her. There is blood on his shirt from a hole in his chest, and Jonathan fears the man is dying. The scene is sad but beautiful, and he hopes that someday he might die as gallantly and bravely as this cowboy.

Playtime

They have climbed to the top of the hill across the street. Looking down, their house appears small and the roof of the mill becomes a patchwork puzzle of shapes and forms. Jonathan tries to find the two trees that hold the rope swings from which, minutes earlier, they had been swinging, jungle-fashion, one to the other, but the green leaves are too dense. Behind him is the shell of a house under construction.

"Why did we come up here?" he asks.

Joe expands, clownlike, his face lit with its friendliest smile. "You want to play cowboys, don't you?"

Jonathan nods his head, grateful that they have accepted him as a playmate, but, when Teddy takes him by the arm and urges him toward the house, he balks.

"I'm scared."

"Nobody's going to hurt you," Joe says cheerfully.

"Come on," Teddy mumbles, "you're the bad guy. We're just going to tie you up."

With some trepidation, he climbs through the window ahead of them. Once inside, the good guys move quickly, making him lie on the floor. Teddy ties Jonathan's hands behind his back, then wraps the rest of the

25

clothesline around his ankles and draws them up to his hands, bending his spine painfully backwards in the process.

"It hurts," he protests meekly.

"Don't worry. I'll untie you in a minute," Teddy assures him.

The two older boys leave to explore other rooms but, before they can return, footsteps are heard and they make their escape through the nearest window, abandoning Jonathan to pain and martyrdom.

The doorknob turns and the door swings open. Footsteps slowly approach. Jonathan hopes he will not be blamed for being there, that whoever is coming will understand that he did not do this to himself, or that Joe and Teddy will return to explain his plight; but they have already fled to safer ground.

His back is to the doorway but he hears the footsteps stop suddenly, then a sharp whistle. Strong, steady hands untie him, then lift him to his feet, but he is afraid to look up at the face. The hands guide him out through the door to safety. As he races down the hill, he breathes easier, hearing no shouted threat to tell his father.

Short Pants

Mother made a pair of short pants. Jonathan had not been aware of this as he sat listening to her pump the treadle of the sewing machine. Only when she had him strip to his underwear and stand atop a dining room chair for a fitting did he realize what she had been doing. Before she could slip the pants onto him, however, a lady appeared in the doorway and Mother invited her in. Those two became involved in a friendly conversation, during which Mother displayed her handiwork before finally dressing her son, and the lady cheerfully remarked what a big boy he was.

Meanwhile, Jonathan was held in the grip of embarrassment. It was not right for the lady to see him that way, and even after he was safely within the protective confines of the brown shorts, he felt the glaring nakedness of his legs. He wished that the lady would go away, that he would never again have to wear short pants.

Two Girls

Caroline lives in the house where the road bends, across the street from the well. One day, she visits Jonathan while he is playing on the terrace. Nothing of consequence happens. There is no memorable conversation or action, only a mutual sense of wonder at each other's existence and a feeble sharing of knowledge that each is somehow important to the other. The experience and its possibilities are short-lived, however, as Caroline is soon called home and Jonathan must content himself with watching her lithe body scamper up the bank, golden hair flapping with her movements and her short dress trying to tell him something. He finds her admirable and hopes she will come back again someday.

She doesn't.

Gloria is perhaps a year younger than Jonathan. Her family is visiting this day. She has fallen and sits, unattended for the moment, on the gravel parking space in front of the house. Because her legs are spread apart and her underpants are in disarray, pebbles and grit get caught in the crack of her behind and she starts bawling, then keeps bawling until rescue and comfort arrive.

28

Once again, Jonathan has noticed something that barely touches the edge of his consciousness, that struggles to tug at a nerve but loses its grip to fall away into dark recesses where it lies moaning, grumbling to be set free; crawls through dark tunnels of membrane in its effort to resurface into the light of consequence.

Jonathan merely scratches his head at the girl's plight, wondering if he is missing something.

Willie

Willie went to court one day to be a witness against a man who tried to make a second-grade girl ride in his truck. When Willie came home, he excitedly told Jonathan, "The sheriff let me hold his pistol."

Jonathan was astounded by his brother's good luck, but also jealous. He wondered if fate would ever be as kind to him.

Malfeasance

It is Sunday morning and the family has scattered to different interests. Joe and Teddy are in the kitchen; Jonathan is on the living room floor deeply absorbed in the comics; Mother is in her bedroom, occupied with some chore. Father has just arrived home from dropping Willie and Sis off at Sunday school. Jonathan hears him enter the kitchen and say to the two boys, "Here. I bought a quart of soda. Be sure to save some for Jonathan."

A comforting warmth settles into his system because Father has remembered him and has ordered his brothers to remember him also. Feeling assured that the treat will be there when he is ready for it, he continues his perusal of the comics, conceiving his own storylines from the pictures. By the time he descends the stairs to the kitchen, Father has once again left the house and the boys are at the table playing cards.

"Where's mine?" he asks.

"Where's your what?" Joe replies disinterestedly as he studies his cards.

"My soda." Something wavers on the precipice of his world, about to topple down on him with Father no longer there to restore the damage or make things right.

"There isn't any left."

Jonathan stands gaping at his brothers. He sees their minds switch him off and they are no longer aware of his existence. He wants to scream at them but is afraid of their wrath, wants to cry but knows that their hearts are too cold to be scorched by tears, wishes that Father would return to administer justice but realizes that they would not have been miscreant had he been within calling distance, wishes that Mother could be convinced of their evil ways but Joe has always been her favorite and Jonathan does not know the right words with which to plead his case.

He suffers in silence, too stunned to cry and too ignorant to speak, vowing he will never forget what they have done to him.

And yet another Sunday morning over the comics: colors brighten the tunnels in Jonathan's mind; stories form around the many characters; jokes and puns abound and villains get their comeuppance. As these delights touch his fancy, Joe and Teddy enter the room, snatch the comics away from him and settle down to enjoy them.

He is enraged. He screams, cries, stamps his feet, demands the return of the comics to their rightful per-user, grabs for them but is pushed away. The histrionics continue in the hope that justice will arrive and prevail, but when Father does come, it is Jonathan who receives the beating and is ordered to behave properly.

The child believes that what has happened is not fair, but he is afraid to say so. Through tears, he glares at his brothers who, in return, ignore him. This does not seem right, either, and a dark, powerful feeling, one that he has never experienced before, fills his mind. The feeling both astounds and frightens him, and he is not even aware that it has a name.

The Kite

Jonathan is on his hands and knees. He has taken the slats from two old window shades and tied them together to form a cross. Some string is fastened into notches on the ends of both sticks so that each end is connected to its neighbors. This framework is laid on top of a sheet from the Sunday comics. With a pair of scissors, he trims away about an inch beyond the string, folds the paper over the string and tapes it. A tail of old rags is fastened to the bottom of the cross, a piece of string attached to the arms so that it hangs loosely and the end of the ball of string is tied to the middle.

There is a strong breeze. As Jonathan lifts the kite, he feels it pulling up away from him, anxious to soar. He runs up the road toward the mill, letting out string as he goes, and the kite rises. He glances back over his shoulder at the miracle he has wrought.

This happy moment becomes frozen, the broad smile on his face fixed forever. The laughter in his eyes has solidified into a piercing note for all time. Inside his mind, eternal now, a sense of himself soaring. The kite hangs at its apex, caught by the sun and set ablaze in a glorious burst of colors.

33

Then the frozen moment is suddenly shattered. The sky darkens. The kite disappears into a mass of leaves and branches. The string breaks and falls limply to the ground. For a long while, Jonathan's mind continues its flight without him, then realizes it is outside where it does not belong and returns to him. Back inside, it becomes aware of the green canopy high above his head and the short piece of string dangling from an unseen source and swinging in the breeze.

Jonathan does not know how to feel, amazed by his brief accomplishment or disappointed over his loss.

First Grade Dropout

Clutching his lunchbox for the first time, his mind dwells briefly on its tinny smell and the comforting odor of peanut butter sandwiches coming from within. He walks timidly behind Sis and the others, his reluctance drawing their ire. Workmen help them across a walkway on the partially built new metal bridge, then it is back to the old sluggish pace. They pass a coal pile, mill houses extending back along a lane toward the cliff above the creek, a store at the bottom of a hill, a farm with an apple orchard running upward to the state highway and the school on the opposite side.

The building is huge and imposing from the outside; a fenced-in playground surrounds it. The inside is even more imposing. A wide hallway leads to a stairwell and fifth, sixth, seventh, and eighth graders can be seen climbing to their rooms.

Then, before he realizes what is happening, Sis's fingers dig into his back; she leans over his shoulders and whispers, "In there," and he finds himself abandoned in a doorway. A voice, harsh and grating, comes from an elderly woman sitting behind a desk halfway across a room full of children. "Come here! Come in! Don't just stand there."

Jonathan spins around, seeking help from Sis but she is gone. Again the voice comes out to him, coldly demanding, "I said get in here."

As he has already been programmed to do, Jonathan obeys this grownup. He marches stiff-legged into the room and stops by the side of the desk. The silence is ominous. His eyes flicker momentarily, and his gaze rises to her countenance just long enough to cause him to recoil in fright.

"What's your name?" she demands.

The words strike him like blows. He realizes that he is expected to respond, but he has never had the experience and does not know how. He senses fury building within her and tries to reply before she can vent it, but his mind malfunctions, leaving him with a trembling of lips that spreads to his entire body.

"I asked you what your name is," she says impatiently.

He captures the words in his lungs, sucking them in with a deep breath, but is unable to expel them. Finally, he breathes in as much air as he can, then blows the name imperfectly out at her, "J- J- J- J- Jonathan!" This accomplished, he finds himself breathing heavily as tears fill his eyes.

To his relief, she ignores his ineptitude and points to an unoccupied desk in the middle of the room. He walks to it, noticing, as he passes, faces staring unhappily down at the desktops. Sliding onto his seat, he places the lunchbox on the floor, then hears the gruff voice call his name. Looking up, he sees a frown more horrible than he ever thought possible.

"You are to keep your eyes on your desktop. You are not to look around or talk to anyone. You are not to look up or speak unless I tell you to. If you disobey, you will be punished."

Again, meekly and obediently, Jonathan does as he is told, but only for a while. He recalls being told that Willie would be in the same room with him, though in another grade, and he looks around for his brother, hoping for at least some moral support, but he is unable to find him in the confusing sea of faces.

A loud smacking sound sends him bouncing on his buttocks, spinning forward in his seat, and he finds himself staring up into the loathing eyes of Miss Merriman; remembering, with growing terror, what Willie had told him about her. She is tapping a ruler against her hand, speaking sharply and cruelly; "Hold your hand out."

Jonathan obeys.

"Palm up!"

He blinks in incomprehension.

Miss Merriman takes his hand and flips it over, then taps the correct part with the ruler. "This is your palm. The next time you disobey me you will be struck hard with the ruler." She hits the desktop with it, and it makes the same loud noise he had heard before. "Do you understand me?"

He nods his head.

"You do not nod your head to me; you speak. If you understand what I just told you, tell me so."

Jonathan is aware of strain in his eyes, of moisture filming over them, of his wide-open mouth which he cannot close. "Uh- uh- uh- "

Her gaze holds on him for a long time. Finally, she spins away and hurries back along the aisle toward her desk. "The next time I talk to you, you had better be prepared to answer me."

He glances across the room, his attention drawn there by some instinct, and sees Willie glaring at him in disgust, then his brother averts his eyes in embarrassment.

During the day, he constantly finds his attention wandering for brief moments: when Miss Merriman is busy instructing the second grade or intimidating one of his fellow first-graders; when the recess bell rings for the upper-graders and they come stamping down the stairs past his classroom doorway. Only once more is he caught but is spared the ruler. He is relieved when the final bell rings and he finds Sis at the door waiting for him.

The next day, he explains to Mother that he does not want to return to school, but she ignores his whining and once again thrusts the lunchbox at him, directing him to go with Sis and Willie.

All of the students have crowded into the seventh and eighth grade classroom to hear the principal, Mr. Oetker, deliver a lecture on obeying rules. Before he speaks, he takes roll call. When Jonathan's name is called, he raises his hand, as the others have done before him, but his presence is not acknowledged. A long silence follows. He lifts himself from the seat so he can peek over the top of the desk and discovers Mr. Oetker searching for him among the tightly packed students, a look of perturbation on his face. Jonathan waves his hand, hoping to gain the man's attention.

At the same time, the eighth grader sitting beside him raises his hand and says, "Here he is," and points down at his seatmate. Mr. Oetker's gaze finally falls on Jonathan. A grin cracks his face, then he joins the entire school in laughter. Jonathan manages a faint smile, knowing that the joke is really on him, knowing that it has saved him from the stern principal's wrath.

He has a chance meeting with Mr. Oetker in the boys' room. They are sitting on commodes, diagonally across from each other in the dim light.

Mr. Oetker says, "You're Jonathan, aren't you?"

"Yes." The reply is barely more than a whisper, but he is proud that he has so quickly learned not to nod his head at questioners.

"Are you a good boy?"

"Yes."

"Fine. Fine. Don't be a troublemaker like your brothers."

Jonathan does not know what a troublemaker is, so he says nothing.

"They're always getting into fights."

"I don't fight," Jonathan says truthfully, though it does not occur to him that this might be so only because the opportunity has never presented itself.

"Good. Good."

Mr. Oetker smiles, and Jonathan is sure the man

likes him. This makes him feel happy.

A child who violates any of Miss Merriman's rules may be made to sit in front of the room facing the rest of the class. If the principal happens to enter while this punishment is being enforced, the child is guaranteed a beating. The possibility of this happening is very much on Jonathan's mind one morning as he sits facing his classmates in front of the blackboard, the center of everyone's attention.

And it does happen: the door swings open and Mr. Oetker struts into the room. Jonathan's head snaps up and his mouth falls open; he is unable to control his fear as he stares up at the man's impassive face. But Mr. Oetker walks past him to snatch another boy from behind his desk, then bends him over a seat in front of the room. A rubber hose, appearing as if by magic, is slapped again and again against the boy's bottom. Finally, with no sound having been made during the entire incident, the boy returns to his desk with tears dripping down his cheeks. Mr. Oetker straightens his plump body, nods his head at Miss Merriman, then struts back past Jonathan and out of the room.

He wishes that Miss Merriman would like him but she maintains a level of malevolence that strikes continuous fear in him and causes his stuttering to worsen. She scolds him for failing to pay attention, for fidgeting, for looking up from his desk to watch the older children rush past the door on their way to the playground. She insults him, berates him, but cannot make him understand what school is all about. He wishes he could please her, wishes he could change. She keeps him after school as punishment but even this has no effect. After one particularly trying day, when they are alone in the room, she ties a bright red ribbon in his blond hair and calls him a girl.

When Joe comes to take him home that afternoon, he notices the ribbon and bursts out laughing. Miss Merriman also finds it funny, a delightful joke, and she laughs, sending chills of humiliation through Jonathan.

39

He does not speak during the homeward journey but later, when Joe passes the story on, Jonathan is forced to give the details. He stutters so badly that Father becomes annoyed and, realizing this, the boy becomes completely unable to communicate.

"Stop stuttering!" Father says. "It sounds terrible. Now, tell me what happened at school."

"B-B-But..." He wants to explain but can't.

"I said stop it!"

Jonathan shrugs his shoulders and finds that this alleviates the pressure somewhat. He repeats the act several times, then quickly says, "I-I-d-d-don't know."

By now, Father is exasperated. "Stop that! Why are you shrugging your shoulders?"

"W-W-What?"

"You're going like this." Father mimics Jonathan's movements, adding contorted facial expressions. "It looks ugly."

Jonathan does not join the other children in play during recess but wanders about the schoolyard. He hears shouting and laughter but does not know how to become part of it, or even if he is supposed to. Since no one has ordered him to participate in the play, he is left to decide, on his own, if he is obligated to do so or if he even has the prerogative of choice; he only knows he does not have the capacity to reach conclusions. He does not want to do the wrong thing and thus incur Miss Merriman's wrath.

While he is pondering these matters, the bell rings ending recess, but lost in thought as he is, he does not hear it and finds himself alone in the schoolyard, watching the door close behind the last of the children. Panic sets in. It is too late to return to the classroom without being punished, and he cannot stay in the schoolyard for the same reason.

This time, Jonathan does not ponder alternatives. He hurries out through the open gateway, crosses the highway and runs down the hill, past the coal pile and into a dense fog, slows to catch his breath as he nears the bridge but spies the headlights of a car coming up behind him and quickens his pace again. His feet pound against the newly finished metal bridge. He knows if he can make it to the other side, they will not be able to catch him and inflict on him whatever horrible torture they have in mind.

He is across, and the car turns the other way up the steep, winding hill past the papermill and the boss's mansion. Safe, he slows to a trot, then walks, in what he hopes is a calm manner, into the house and down the stairs to Mother's side.

A look of astonishment forms on her face, but her voice is steady as she asks, "What are you doing home so early?"

"I don't feel good."

She accepts his clever answer without further comment, but shortly thereafter, she agrees with Mr. Oetker's suggestion that he be kept home until the next school year.

Epilogue 3

The children are playing in a park. They are running and laughing. The girl is with them but, out in the sunshine, she is no longer dark and frightening. Little Boy enjoys being with her and laughing with her. They lead the children to a high cliff at the edge of the park, holding their hands so they won't fall.

War!

It is nighttime and the family has gathered in the kitchen. The shades have been pulled down so the dimmed light of the kerosene lamp will not be seen by the pilots of enemy bombers, and everyone speaks in whispers so spies will not overhear them. An air-raid warden patrols the village streets, making sure the blackout rules are obeyed. Jonathan worries not only that their house might be bombed because their light is too bright or because someone speaks too loudly, but that they will all be sent to jail for these violations; that they will be put to shame because of their carelessness. Still, it is nice having the family together in this little room where everyone is so close that each can reach out and touch any of the others, can feel the body heat and warm breath of one another in opposition to the frigid air attacking the world outside. Shadows are soft and slow, making him so drowsy he has to fight to stay awake. He does not want to sleep through this best of times.

Sally

Nobody knew where Sally came from or where she eventually went, but she showed up at the house one day, was fed, and decided to stay on. She had black and gray stripes, was no better than the average cat but was well-loved by the children and by Mother.

One day, Joe and Teddy both decided to play with Sally at the same time. They picked her up but neither was willing to let the other take possession of her, and they argued about this.

"I want to hold Sally," Joe said.

"I want to hold Sally," Teddy said.

Joe held her by the front legs and Teddy by the hind legs. They pulled in opposite directions, tugging with all their might to get her away from each other, each shouting at the other that he had her first. Meanwhile, Sally snarled, hissed, growled, spat, and cried out in pain from being stretched like a rubber band.

Jonathan watched helplessly, unable to speak or move in Sally's defense. Even Sis could do nothing to stop the violence. Then, just when it seemed the cat would be torn in half, Father came bursting out through the doorway already yanking the belt from its loops. The boys let Sally go, then each took a step in the direction of escape, but they were not quick enough.

Sally ran wildly around the corner of the house and down the hill toward the creek. Jonathan and Sis gave chase but were unable to catch her.

This image of the cat stayed in his mind for a long time: the animal writhing and screaming, being twisted and pulled without thought or pity, something savage and beastlike yet noble in her struggle and in her suffering. Later, he would think back on this incident and wonder if it had been the cause of her coming apart.

He did not know how this happened; he only knew that Sally had gotten sick and her belly had swelled like a balloon; then she came apart one day. Vaguely, he thought he remembered seeing her lying in the weeds on the upper bank, making strange noises and movements. Then her stomach opened and her insides came out. Father was there, taking care of Sally and assuring Jonathan that she would be all right.

He believed that Sally did get better, though she hardly ever came to the house after that and spent most of her time at the papermill.

How the Flickering Images. . .

The pictures flashing upon the screen shatter his faith in perpetuity. Warmth oozes out through his pores and cold seeps in. He shivers as a wagon races through a stormy night and a chalk-white corpse bounces again and again against the driver, its arms flopping wildly, and during this time, Jonathan feels his own flesh touching the dead man's flesh and the horror is so great, his breathing becomes labored. The world is a cave here; he is alone inside while evil forces struggle at its entrance, not yet aware of him, but, given time...

Willie and Mother are on the other side of the cave's wall, unable or unwilling to communicate with him, unable even to reach his consciousness. He is alone with wicked men and there is nothing barring their way to him. Joe, Teddy, and Sis have chosen to see Lassie, having gone with Father to the city's other theater. No one will save Jonathan if that dreaded hunger...

The plot does not survive the flickering images. All that has gone before and all that comes after the corpse's eerie ride is of no significance; even the crash of the wagon etches no permanent memory. No; it is only the flopping corpse's snow-white flesh touching...

Until the movie's end, he ponders these things: death, the violent struggle which has brought it about and how terrible it must be to die; how horrible it is to see a dead man and to imagine touching the unimaginable; how frightening it is to hear such evil in a man's voice and to see it in eyes that...

Jonathan hugs himself to subdue the chill.

After the movie, he and Willie escort Mother through the glittering city to rejoin the rest of the family. They find them already in the car, which is parked on a side street. Father flicks on the interior light as they climb in, and Jonathan settles down between him and Mother.

"How was the movie?" Father asks, showing a rare smile.

Jonathan gazes up at his face, happy that he has cared enough to ask. "Good," he replies softly.

Joe leans forward from the back seat and grins down at him. "How did you like Boris Karloff?"

Jonathan squints, trying to remember who Boris Karloff was in the movie. "Good," he says, hoping that is the correct answer.

Joe's laughing face falls away and is replaced by Sis's; kindly smiling. "Were you scared?"

He shakes his head, glances up to see if Mother will contradict him, but the light is turned off and her face becomes unfathomable in the darkness.

The headlights go on and soon the car is moving homeward.

First Grade

Once again, it is across the bridge, past the coal pile and the millhouses, past the store and up the hill to school. Miss Merriman is still there, as mean and cranky as ever but not quite as frightening as before; her attacks on his nerves now don't inspire fits of stuttering; he is able to sit at his desk with almost complete attention focused on the pages of his books.

Older girls fall in love with him. Sis and her friends gather on the porch before and after school. They fuss over Jonathan, combing his hair and remarking on his cuteness, causing Sis to blush with pride. To him, the evidence is overwhelming that girls are nice. He adores them, would side with them in their arguments with boys if he dared speak up, admires Sis's courage when she shouts into the face of a rather hefty older boy, "Sammy Willis, you're a big bag of wind!"

After school, he walks home with Sis. One day, he notices Willie ahead of them with two older boys. An argument is taking place concerning some coins that Willie has in his possession, and suddenly one of the boys tries to take them away from him. Fists fly and the group moves off the road onto a patch of sand. Willie stumbles to the ground and his attackers leap on him.

Sis runs over and tries to pull the boys off her brother. Jonathan is close behind, determined to follow Sis and Willie into oblivion, if necessary, in order to preserve family honor. He lunges into the mass of bodies and swinging arms, hoping only to grasp someone and cling to him so that brother or sister can finish with the culprit. Instead, after a moment of blackness, he finds himself flat on his back in the sand, a short distance from Willie who is in the same position, and, also like Willie, a boy towering over him. Only now does fear flow into his mind, just like the tears filling his eyes. He is enraged by the injustice which is occurring, helpless to do anything about it. Vaguely, he hears Sis pleading on their behalf but it is obvious these evil children will show no mercy.

The boy bends down; the despicable face comes closer. Suddenly, a bit of action catches Jonathan's attention. Willie has flung a handful of sand into the face of his antagonist, causing that bully to stumble backwards, sputtering and spitting and wiping his eyes. Then, as if on its own volition, Jonathan's hand digs into the sand. Without thought and with only a semi-conscious need for self-preservation, he flings the sand upward into his bully's face and sees him back off, sputtering and spitting and wiping his eyes just like the other.

During this brief diversion, Jonathan, Willie, and Sis make their escape.

Eventually, he is allowed to walk home alone. He does this with a sense of wonder, walking slowly and exploring the roadside environment. Once, he discovers an empty soda bottle which he takes into the store. He places the bottle atop the counter, then studies the variety of sweets. Finally, after being told what his money can purchase, he points at a pack of gum. The storekeeper reaches in and takes the pack out, breaks it open and hands him one stick. Jonathan hurries from the store excitedly clutching his prize.

In the millhouse lane live several wicked boys; they swear, have bad manners, steal, are nasty, and never take baths. He has learned this from various sources. There is also an old lady there, someone mean and unpleasant who is always sitting in the front window of her house and glaring out at people, sometimes raising a horn to her ear whenever some person inside speaks to her. Across the street from the coal pile, in another millhouse, lives a negro named Lolly. Lolly is, according to Father, a good nigger who is always cheerful and kind and who knows his place.

Sometimes Willie and Jonathan stop at the mill after school to search for treasure or to simply lie atop the huge scrap bundles, many of which are wrapped in war posters, and watch the men with their magnificent machines as they construct the new sawdust building up the hill above them.

One day, Jonathan discovers a book of wallpaper samples. The colors and patterns are so beautiful that he takes the collection home as a surprise for Mother. Instead of thanks or words of praise, however, he is scolded and cannot understand why.

These things seem to him to be all that is worth remembering about his first year of school, except, perhaps, Dick, Jane, and Spot. Soon it is over. In the spring, he receives a card stating that he has passed to the second grade. Willie goes to fourth grade, Sis to sixth grade, and Teddy to seventh. Joe graduates to high school and is given an American flag at the ceremonies as a citizenship award.

New Home

That summer, Father loaded a truck with the family possessions, with Mother and the children, and drove north for one mile to their new home, which neighbored Grandma's house. Uncle Lou had gone off to war, Aunt Jane had gotten a job in a factory, the other uncles and aunts had married and moved away. The move was made so Mother could look after Grandma who was over eighty years of age.

Although the new home looked very old and dilapidated, it was actually fairly new and dilapidated. It had been built but never finished by relatives who had argued over its construction. Like the old home, it had no running water, but it did have electricity. Windows were out of line and the building tilted to the right; the weather-beaten exterior had never been touched by paint. The floors sloped in many directions. A cellar had been started but never completed, leaving only a hole in the ground beneath the front of the house and a dirt crawl space elsewhere, with light shining through gaps in what should have been a foundation, while various pieces of lumber, bricks, cinder blocks, and other scraps were used as columns to brace the floor. The brick chimney here was crooked with bulges, giving the impression of imminent collapse, and this aspect remained through the length of its ascension.

A dirt driveway ran along the front of the house to a decaying wooden porch. Over the front door hung a horseshoe. The door opened to the kitchen with its combination wood/coal stove, a washstand and a floor cabinet with two water buckets atop it, an old bucket serving as a garbage pail, a space for firewood, and a corner for the broom and mop. The front window looked out over the cellar door, while the side window looked out at the nearby woods.

The dining room was off the kitchen. The Kalamazoo stove was here, beneath a vent to the second floor. In the room were a round table, its extra leaves tucked away in a corner, a dish closet and a sideboard. One window looked out at the driveway and two others at the side lawn, the road, and an apple orchard beyond. A wide doorway led to the living room with its couch, two easy chairs, a bookcase holding a set of encyclopedias, and a radio. Two windows looked out on the lawn, road, and orchard and the rear window at a plot of ground which would become a garden. A door from the living room led to a bedroom, as did one from the kitchen, and to the passageway to the second floor, but this consisted only of a ladder until Father built a staircase.

All the floors upstairs were bare and uneven, as were most of the walls. One bedroom was at the top of what came to be the stairwell. It was the largest and most open of the bedrooms, all of which changed occupants frequently, and had one window which looked out over the back garden plot and the hilltop pasture of the neighboring farm. The inner walls were unpapered and composed of a soft substance which could take no punishment. One piece of this wallboard was nailed to the ceiling beams where a light fixture was located. Opposite this was a small room with a window and a doorway to a closet which overhung the stairwell. Another doorway in the closet led to Willie's and Jonathan's room. This had a window overlooking the cellar door, the main lawn, and a Greening apple tree between their house and

Grandma's; a patch of wallboard for the light and, also like the other bedrooms, no ceiling; only empty space beneath the rafters and leaky roof. The naked, lumpy chimney ran up the wall near the doorway. A small board was missing from the floor at the entrance, extending under the wall to a ledge over the stairs; here Willie and Jonathan hid their treasures and mice made entrances and exits. The last room, behind a single layer of that same wallboard, had a window with a view similar to theirs.

The woods began behind the house, running down into a deep valley which the creek flowed through, surrounding fenced-in pastureland cut by a stream. Where an upper bank stretched toward flat ground beyond the end of the driveway, hidden by lilacs and other bushes, there was the family dump, a can's throw from the front porch. An outhouse sat on a wood foundation at the top of the bank above thick growths of nettle. Near the outhouse was an open-ended shed used mostly for storage. There was a cistern behind Grandma's house, the water used for washing dishes, scrubbing floors, and personal cleanliness. A well for drinking water was located beyond Grandma's, far down the hill. There were more lilacs on the main lawn and an apple tree on either side of the driveway between the house and the road. Beside the road, towering over everything in sight, was the biggest oak tree Jonathan would ever see.

Epilogue 4

Little Boy has gone deep into the woods to look for Simon. His task is very difficult because Simon is a mute. He had not been born that way; someone had cut off his tongue. No one knows who did this, but everyone believes there was a sinister reason behind it.

Something compels Little Boy to look up. He sees a tightly packed grove of trees and realizes that he has gone too far. This is a forbidden part of the forest. And, high up in one tree, dangling from a rope, he sees the body of a man hanging limply in the still air. The rope is around the man's neck. His eyes are wide-open, his swollen tongue protruding. Over a period of time the sun has baked the skin a grayish-brown color.

Despite the stillness, Little Boy feels shadows cross over him to blot out the sun. The light dims and dark spirits reach out for him, moving through the branches and leaves. Terrified, he hurries away from the place.

But he stops. Lying in the path is a severed head. He stands there in shock, speechless, pointing at the grotesque thing. He senses danger, the presence of someone watching him from the grove of trees. Little Boy is aware of his helplessness, that he is at that person's mercy. He knows that the person possesses evil power, but still feels that the man himself might not be evil, that he might even be hoping he will not have to hurt Little Boy.

"Daddy,

do you remember that day you picked me up and your hand accidentally slid in where it shouldn't have been, and the flicker in your eyes was as brief as the shivering thrill that cut through me and as permanent as the confusion of its aftertaste, and then you said you wouldn't carry me up the stairs to my bed anymore because I was getting too big?"

Zombie!

Jonathan is in a man's house, in a dark room. A thin line of light slips in under the door and flows across the patterned linoleum to the far corner. His father and the man are talking in the next room, so low he cannot understand what they say.

In the faint light, in a corner, is the zombie. It comes toward him, walking slowly, a knife clutched in its hand. Dead eyes stare at him, coldly yet with intimated hunger.

"Daddy!" he yells but gets no response.

Jonathan tries to scamper to his feet and run but keeps slipping on the slick linoleum and cannot move. As the zombie comes closer, the panic grows until Jonathan becomes dizzy with fear. Already, he feels the blade sinking into his chest, the bursting of his heart and his body convulsed by unbearable pain.

"Daddy! Daddy!"

But the men continue their conversation as though they hadn't heard him.

"Daddy!" he screams. He knows he is about to die and nobody cares. In the middle of his last scream, he awakens, gasping for breath as tears fill his eyes. He still feels the presence of the zombie and of death. He whimpers to the darkness, "Why won't he come?," then drifts back to sleep.

Swimming Holes

There is a swimming hole where the creek is about to leave their property. The water here is deep and calm, the bank dropping off sharply. A fallen tree lies beneath the surface a third of the way to the other side and unknown creatures make it their home. Joe, Teddy, Cousin Bob and their braver friends dive from this and, later, after they have learned to swim, so do Willie and Jonathan.

Just south of their property, a bed of rock lies in the creek. Like two more beyond it, this bed extends nearly to the opposite shore. It is fairly jagged, containing small pools and rocks where the boys sometimes hunt dobsons for fishing. The bank becomes smooth beyond this, the shoreline slope less inclined and the water more shallow. A hundred feet or so brings a sharp rise in the bank where the ground is broken away and tree roots are exposed above rich clay, leading to the second bed of rock. The rockbed and clay are the same dark-gray color. This bed is flat and the children stretch out on it in the sun. The rock dips into the water for a good distance northward and here Jonathan learns to swim by pushing himself along on his fingertips, farther and farther out until he is dogpaddling, swallowing scum and loudly kicking sprays of water into the air.

The bed sinks just past the center, then rises again. A pool is trapped here, only inches deep, home for dozens of minnows. A large rock, about Jonathan's height, rests incongruously near shore where the bed slopes back into the water as though it had been plucked from some mountain and laid there by the hand of a giant. The bed extends to the opposite shore, but the far side is under water whenever the gate in the dam at the northern end of town is opened. Usually, however, there are swift currents through channels in the moss-covered rocks, forming a natural slide for a long ride downstream.

The current is visible almost as far as the last bed of rock, a humpbacked peninsula which none of the boys dares to swim to because of unseen life forms, particularly a nest of snakes, which are rumored to dwell there in the shade of an elm.

The children struggle up the base of a hill that climbs past the rockbeds. Beneath a broiling sun, they pass through a barbed wire fence, then follow a path still upward through the woods. Somewhere short of the waterwell at the bottom of the final hill, a girl faints and the older children gather around her to render assistance. She is a teenager, a friend of Cousin Annie who, with Joe, informs everyone there that she had suffered a heat stroke and will have to rest awhile. A blanket is placed on the ground; the girl sits on it, her skin almost white in the surrounding shade. Jonathan stares at her drained but pretty face, hoping she will not die.

Second Grade

Jonathan's new school is situated along a gravel lane connected to one of the village's quiet streets. It rests at the end of some level ground atop a hill. The village's shale-roofed firehouse is across the lane. On its second floor, there is an auditorium and a stage with rich red curtains. In front of the firehouse is the lower grades' ballfield with a chainlink fence bordering first base. The fence extends past a shallow outfield and clay tennis court beyond it, turning north past the court and the upper grades' ballfield and descending a slope to another gravel lane. This lane, which eventually crosses the other at the bottom of the hill, dips to join the main street where there is a bridge high above the rocky creek.

The middle grades' ballfield is on the northside of the school, sharing part of the upper grades' outfield; its third base a mere fifteen feet from home plate because of the lane and its left field dropping steeply away from the rest of the outfield. First base is far from home to compensate for third but close to second which is a telephone pole. Third base on the upper grades' diamond is nearly aligned with its home plate and the first base of the middle grades' diamond. Second base is also close to first on that diamond, atop the hill where it curves and beyond which outfielders lose sight of home plate. Second base on the lower grades' diamond is fairly moveable but third base is a maple tree.

The school itself is somewhat like Jonathan's old one but made of brick. There is a bell tower in the center of the roof. A cable from this hangs through a hole in the seventh/eighth-grade ceiling. It is the goal of nearly every lower-grade boy to someday pass into the seventh grade to have a chance to be designated official bell ringer. The other room on the second floor houses the fifth and sixth grades, which is directly above the room for the third and fourth grades. The first two grades are on the first floor.

Jonathan's teacher is a young, pretty woman. Her name is Mrs. Johnson. Her gentle ways make learning more fun than it had been under Miss Merriman and not at all frightening. He quickly learns, however, that there are enough tyrants in his grade to more than compensate for the loss of his former teacher; two boys in particular, Frankie, the bully, and his companion, James, who have taken it upon themselves to rule the playground during recess, lunch period, and after school, extending their authority to the village streets or to wherever they happen to come across other boys from the class. During the fall season, Jonathan finds himself being challenged often and rolling in the dirt with his tormentors with results that are always positive, yet negative in the sense that each victory only serves to draw new attacks from two boys with whom he would rather be friends. He sometimes wishes he could take their bullying as passively as the other boys do but feels that this would only serve to dishonor his family.

His best friend is Ernest, a first grader who lives on a farm a half-mile down the road from his house. Ernest has golden hair which falls in ringlets down to his shoulders and clear blue eyes which are often filled with tears because the other boys call him a girl and a sissy. Jonathan often finds himself staring with pity across the room at the boy. He is glad that his friend's mother has not had the heart to cut her son's hair; he thinks Ernest is beautiful and should remain that way. They walk home together after school, Jonathan offering encouragement and sympathy, but the friendship is short-lived because Ernest's parents leave the farm late in the fall and move to another town.

There are no girls in the second grade, but there are six other boys, each with his own fault: Frankie and James; Andy, who tells smutty jokes; Fred with his sour disposition and high opinion of himself; Donald, who swears and likes to quarrel about almost everything; and Sammy, who is dumb but otherwise okay. Sammy lives across the creek beside the state highway, too far away to be a real friend. Nor are there any older boys, including Cousin Bob who swears too much and is bossy, for him to admire. Mostly, all that the older boys like to do is show off in front of girls and run around trying to rip one another's fly open. The worst offender in this business is Ox, the overgrown son of a farmer, who is far more serious about the game than seems reasonable and who Jonathan learns to avoid. Even brother Teddy is a disappointment, being bad-tempered and quick to fight both fellow students and teachers. Willie, too, believes that fighting is important, that no challenge should be allowed to go unmet.

The Word

One day, as Jonathan was walking home from school, a big black dog approached and began sniffing his body. The dog moved around behind him, raised its front paws off the ground and laid them across his shoulders. Jonathan felt the dog's body push up against his, then move rapidly back and forth. He sensed a craziness in the dog's head, something hot and fierce boiling through its blood and into its brain, itching like poison ivy, and this frightened him.

Jack, an older boy, came up beside him, laughing as he said, "He's trying to fuck you."

The word was both sharp and blunt, cutting through him with cold indifference, as though the dog's teeth had sunk into his brain, as black and as chilling as the dog itself and equally frightening.

Jonathan wondered if the word had a precise meaning. If it had, he reasoned, he could learn to avoid it or even fight and conquer it, but not knowing worried him greatly and made him its prisoner. It was such a powerful word, he knew there was only one person strong and wise enough to define it and to drive away the spell it had cast over him.

Early that evening, as the family prepared for supper, he asked, "Daddy, what does fuck mean?"

Instead of the calm, rational explanation he had expected, Father's face went livid with rage. The man raised his fist as if to strike him but banged it against the tabletop instead, then, leaning forward, angrily said, "Don't ever let me hear you say that word again."

Jonathan backed away, too stunned to speak, knowing that everyone else in the family had heard his stupid mistake. He felt humiliated. Still, the angry response hadn't seemed fair, and he wondered if he could ever again trust Father to do the right thing.

Sleeping in Winter

On winter nights, Willie and Jonathan rush on tiptoe into their bedroom, sometimes pausing to hug the
warm chimney beside the bed, then dive beneath the
covers and shiver until their body heat drives out the
cold. They snuggle up to each other in fetal position,
one warming his frontside against the other's backside,
then changing positions, until sleep comes. Often, they
have shouting contests with Joe and Teddy, both sides
calling for their little dog, Brownie, to come warm their
beds, leaving the bewildered animal torn between loyal-
ties. When they win, Brownie slips between them beneath the blanket, stays there awhile, then crawls to the
end of the bed to warm their feet. Sometimes, Jonathan
inadvertently kicks her during the night, gets painfully
nipped, then has to forgive and comfort the whining
pooch. In the morning, the boys leap from the bed, then
race downstairs to dress behind the warming stove.

Shopping

Father has many friends in the city. They call him by name, shake his hand, ask about his family and offer him the best deals around. It makes Jonathan feel good inside to know how respected and admired Father is by all these nice people. He is sure that, because of Father, these feelings are also directed at the rest of the family.

Outside, the street and the stores are decorated with pretty lights in various colors. Santa Claus is also there, greeting passersby with a cheerful, "Ho, Ho, Ho!", and ringing his bell. Jonathan gazes timidly up at him but is not seen. He hopes the jolly man will not be so careless on Christmas morning.

While the other children go elsewhere with Father, Jonathan follows Mother into a five-and-dime. Here, an entire new world opens to him. There are endless lines of counters filled with the most wonderful things he has ever seen: airplanes, guns, trucks, teddy bears, brilliant jewels and other glittering items. People are walking up and down the aisles, handling the toys and games that he is only allowed to look at.

"Mommy!" he says with great excitement on discovering a magnificent firetruck parked inside a glass case,

"Will you buy that for me?" She doesn't reply but tugs at his arm, pulling him back to her side. There is a game in a box. "Mommy!" Before he can ask for it, she tugs him elsewhere. He sees row upon row of candy, more kinds than he has ever seen before and each kind more tempting than its neighbor. "Mommy, can I have some candy?" He is taken past another counter where more items delight his senses, but his pleas for crayons, coloring books, watercolors, and chalk bring not one word from her.

At one point, Mother lets go of his hand to examine some merchandise. Jonathan's attention remains focused on toys but the good manners he has been taught prevent him from handling them. He does not know how long he stands in that spot, but when he turns to take Mother's hand, she is gone.

Angry because of his constant begging, she has abandoned him, left him to the specters of his imagination, to wander the streets alone.

His first steps are taken almost unconsciously, but, when she does not appear beyond the first corner, panic sets in. The pace increases to a near trot. Something hot and heavy crushes in on him; tears fill and burn his eyes and flow down his cheeks in torrents. "Mommy!" he cries, but there is no reply. A lady smiles down at him but offers no assistance. "Mommy!" he yells, knowing she is gone from his life forever, that she and the others will not even miss him. "Mommy! Mommy!" An aisle, lined with living bodies, forms ahead of him, faces smiling, and, at the end of it, is Mother, staunchly silent and calm. He runs to her, grabs her arm and clings to it with all his might.

Outside, she crisply informs him, "This is the last time you ever go shopping with me."

This is fine with him. He does not think he has it in himself to ever go through this kind of experience again.

Ox

Cousin Bob, Teddy, Ox, and some other older boys are wrestling off to the side of the school. A pile of boys forms rapidly, the object being to make it as high as they possibly can. Ox, the biggest and heaviest of the bunch, is stretched out on the side of the pile, bringing groans and laughter from those beneath him. His eyes spot Jonathan who is watching the fun, and he beckons to him.

Jonathan runs as fast as he can and leaps into their midst. His laughter blends with that of the others but only for a moment. He feels a strong hand grasp one of his buttocks, squeezing and twisting as though trying to rip it off, then push hard into the crack. A jolt, like a burst of electricity, shoots through his body, tingling every nerve with a sensation that he suspects is painful. He stiffens with fright, unable to comprehend the feeling that has just exploded within himself, as the hand remains there, tearing him apart. Fright grows to terror as he realizes that his body will not contain that explosion.

With all his might, Jonathan pushes away from the pile, freeing himself from the vise-like grip. He runs several feet away then spins around, intending to hurl words of anger back at the monster, but the words stick in his chest. Just before his eyes flood with tears, he notices Ox gaping at him, face blank and unrepentant.

Jonathan turns and walks slowly over to the swings, realizing with relief that he hasn't been physically injured. But the pain, though he cannot even be sure now that it had been pain he felt, stays with him. He sits on a swing, avoiding eye contact with the nearby children, and spends the remainder of recess wondering what had happened to him and hating Ox.

Ox is sitting behind the steering wheel of his father's parked car. He smiles as Jonathan approaches. "Hi," he says in a friendly manner. "You wanta have some fun?"

"Doing what?"

"Get in. I'll show you."

Obediently, Jonathan walks around to the passenger side and climbs in. He is pleased that the big boy wants to play with him, and already begins to believe he has been wrong about Ox. There is a tenderness in the usually sullen eyes which indicate no harm is intended, a sincere gentleness in the voice which marks him as trustworthy. It is apparent that they are going to take a make-believe car trip.

"Can I have a turn driving?" Jonathan asks hopefully.

Ox shakes his head. "Nah. Let's do something else."

"What?"

"This," Ox says, then proceeds to unbutton his trousers. He takes his penis out. "You wanta suck on it?"

Jonathan studies the fat finger of flesh, wondering how sucking on it could possibly be fun. Considering the organ's function and the probability of contamination by germs, the idea seems preposterous. Afraid he might be hurting his new friend's feelings, he timidly shakes his head.

The feared anger does not surface, however. Instead, Ox smiles understandingly. "That's okay. I'll do it to you." He opens Jonathan's fly, takes his penis out,

70

then leans over, puts it in his mouth and sucks on it. After a few seconds, he tucks it back in, takes his own out again and softly says, "Now, you do it to me."

Again, Jonathan shakes his head. Now that he has had time to think it over, the act seems even more unappealing. He hopes the big boy will stop asking him to do this and will play at pretend driving.

But Ox performs the act on him a second time, takes his own penis out a third time and repeats, "Now, you do it to me." For the third time, the response is a shake of the head.

Ox frowns but, after readjusting their clothing, urges Jonathan out of the car with such a charming manner that the child's conscience is eased. There had been a fear that he'd offended Ox, but now he is happily convinced that they are still friends. And, before shutting the car door, Ox sweetly whispers, "Don't tell anybody what we were doing."

"I won't."

The next time he sees his big friend and says, "Hi!", his cheerful greeting is ignored and Ox pretends he doesn't see him. Jonathan realizes, without any real sense of loss or sadness, that big boys are fickle beyond understanding.

Willie Naked

    One winter morning, Jonathan hurries down the stairs to dress for school. Entering the dining room, he hears a commotion. Willie is standing on a chair in the nook between the stove and far wall without any clothes on and bawling as Mother chastises him. Jonathan does not know what it is all about; doesn't want to know, though he feels certain, because of Willie's red face and damp cheeks, that Mother has struck him. Jonathan stands motionless in front of the warm stove, stunned by the apparent act of violence against his brother and grieving for him, but also embarrassed for Willie because he has let Mother see him naked.

The Outhouse, the Chamber Pot, and Yellow Snow

Jonathan peeks up from the baby seat at Joe and Teddy as they near the end of their comic books. Outside, Cousin Annie is begging them to hurry, but they merely tell her to be patient and continue reading at a sluggish pace. Finally, business finished, they prepare to leave.

"Joe," Jonathan whispers, grinning conspiratorially, "tell Annie to come in."

Joe steps outside. "Okay!" he says cheerfully. "It's all yours."

Teddy steps aside and Cousin Annie appears in the doorway. At first she does not see Jonathan on the low seat in the corner, the grin still on his face. Only when he greets her with a bright, "Hi!", does she notice him. She stops, gasps, blushes, then whirls around with a flutter of her skirt and rushes back outside to scold the boys.

Day turns to night with Jonathan seated over the first of the big folks' accommodations beside the window and facing the half-open door. Moonless, the night is black, the only light creeping in from the distant porch. The wooden seat is sticky and damp from someone's missing the hole earlier, the roll of toilet paper sopping wet; yet his main concern is that one of the huge spiders, whose home this is, will choose this moment to journey across his legs. Also, he must be on the alert for any car which might turn into the driveway, its headlights shining through the open door.

Time quickens to winter. The water from some other nighttime misadventure has turned to ice. His legs are goosebumped and his teeth chatter. A cold wind shakes the outhouse and his fretful mind finds he and building tumbling downhill. These icy visits are infrequent and hasty, but as the snow melts and spring comes, he stays longer, bent over an unending supply of old comic books. Now the problem is the growing pile beneath him, so high he wonders who will be the unlucky one to disrupt it. Sprinklings of lime help temporarily. Then, one day, Father tears off the bottom sideboards and shovels the contents into a deep pit.

Then it is summer again. Jonathan is serenading Mother and Aunt Jane as they hang clothes on the line. When he is done, he pulls his trousers up and flicks the door latch. It is stuck. He pushes against it with his finger but it doesn't move. He lifts, pulls on the door, but nothing happens. He is trapped. Suddenly, the stench overwhelms him, the walls close in and the spiders awaken. He bangs on the door, against the painted letters, "POST NO BILLS", and, bawling, screams, "Mommeeeeee! I can't get out!"

The latch clicks, the door jerks, then swings open. Aunt Jane is there, laughing, then hugging him with forgiveness and encouragement, explaining away his failure as a human being.

The chamber pot sits in the big room at the top of the stairs. It is there for emergency use only; for any child who awakens with a great need in the middle of the night, not for casual use, but its frequent state of fullness indicates that the sternest warning is no match for winter's whistling winds. It must be picked up for use when there is company in the house, otherwise guests can hear the sound in the living room below.

There is the night Mother feeds him, without his knowing, a generous amount of laxative, and he calls for her as his foot feels desperately for the pail in the darkness, fearing its upset, finally finding it with her guidance. And, though darkness provides generous cover, he is constantly aware of light switches and his vulnerability, the possibility of being suddenly thrown into the spotlight. Whenever the pail is light enough, he moves it near the chimney where he is somewhat protected from prying eyes and where he can press his back against the warm bricks, sit comfortably surrounded by musty air and the silence of sleeping people, and make it a pleasant affair.

At times, the pail is too full to use but no one volunteers to empty it. Jonathan will lift the seldom-used lid to be struck by an odor so acrid it brings tears to his eyes. It is no problem in the summer, except that the stench spreads through the upper rooms, but in the winter, he must find his way down the stairs to the front door without injuring himself or awakening anyone, then, dressed only in underwear and barefooted, make as brief an exit as possible to pee off the porch.

Even though this is a rare occurrence, the chamber pot being usable more often than not or his bedsheet getting soaked, one day Father takes him aside for a mild lecture: "I don't want you peeing in the snow anymore. It doesn't look nice, and it's embarrassing when company comes."

Jonathan is about to explain that he is not the only culprit, that dogs and cats also do it, even his brothers, but he knows that Father will not listen. "Okay," he replies, head bowed in just enough shame to cover his guilt, then walks away.

That night, from his window, he contemplates the outhouse by moonlight, feeling the icy seat and the wind rattling the walls, the thick carpet of snow crusted over and a myriad of glistening icycles encasing the apple tree, the infinite wall of blackness rising from the woods and reaching out beyond the stars, and for the first time wonders if life is worth living.

The Ghost

Clouds hid the moon and stars that night. A warm breeze, born in the valley of the woods, brushed across the plane of land surrounding the two houses. The boys ran in various directions while, pressed against a pine at the edge of light from Grandma's porch, Cousin Bob slowly counted aloud. There was laughter as bodies crashed into unseen obstacles or stumbled and fell to the lawn. Then Joe's voice pierced the darkness, calling for a huddle. When they gathered around him, he whispered, "Let's hide in Grandma's cellar."

Jonathan leaped with delight at the suggestion. He ran ahead of the others along the path behind the summer kitchen, past the cistern, around to the side of the porch and into the house. Grandma was in the dining room, sitting at the table, poised with a magnifying glass over her Bible, but she paid them no attention. Jonathan opened the door to the alcove above the cellar. He stepped inside and was about to descend the stairs but stopped so suddenly that Joe and Teddy bumped into him. He gasped and pointed but could not speak or believe his eyes.

Standing at the foot of the stairs was a ghost, or

76

at least something he couldn't describe any other way. A white sheet covered its body, but the most unusual feature was what should have been its head. Attached there, instead, was the globe of a ceiling light, just like those in the village schoolhouse.

The ghost raised an arm beneath the sheet, and its finger pointed at some canning jars on a nearby table, and they went crashing to the floor. At the same instant, the globe-head lit up. The arm swung in a semi-circle, the finger now pointing at a shelf on the opposite wall. Jonathan could not see any jars from his vantage point, but he knew they were there and he could hear them crashing.

He backed out of the alcove, his momentum taking his brothers with him. They said nothing, did not question his behavior, but backed out with him. He closed the door, then led the way out of the house. Jonathan could not bring himself to ask the others what he had seen; he did not know if they had also seen it. They maintained their silence even after returning to the relative safety of the darkness.

Jonathan worried that the ghost might get Grandma, but reflection assured him that God would protect her.

With Willie

Willie and Jonathan build a superhighway beneath the Greening apple tree. They bank mud up in a long line which zigzags and circles back onto itself, then flatten it and wet it with water from an old basin. A gully is dug and a bridge built over it. As this road dries, it hardens. Soon, Willie's truck and Jonathan's car are zooming along with honking horns, revving engines, and screeching brakes, but this wonderland lasts only until the next rainfall.

From creekside, the boys climb up, up, and up to a lush green plateau, wide on its northern end but narrowing to a point in the south, dropping almost straight down on the eastern side, as though some catastrophe had broken off a large chunk, exposing a soft dirt underbelly. This loose dirt extends halfway down the hillside, stops at a narrow cowpath which runs across the face of the cliff to a series of small hills and flats off to the side. A few trees have managed to cling to the section near the base where lies a frog pond with its decaying vegetation and strange odors.

Jonathan gazes up into the bright-blue sky, then

steps out into space. The earth becomes a blur of yellow-brown. It catches him gently but sends him tumbling and sliding down the cliff face amid a cloud of dirt. Then Willie is beside him, on top of him, and they are rolling and falling together as a bundle of laughing bones toward the cowpath. Finally, they stop. Jonathan looks up at tufts of grass which mark the ridge of the cliff's overhang, happy that he has survived another leap. He is sure that he has been brave, because Joe once told them about a woman who had been buried alive there in a landslide and whose body is still in there and has hinted how the same thing could happen at any time to anyone.

After pausing to catch their breaths and regain their senses, he and Willie race down the hill to the frog pond.

"When Mommy told me to kiss her goodnight," Jonathan says as he slides into bed beside Willie, "I told her I was all out of kisses." He giggles at his great cleverness.

"What did she say?"

"Nothing."

They roll over onto their backs and stare up at the rafters, too hot and wide-awake to fall asleep. To start a modicum of air flowing over their bodies, the boys lift the sheet as high as their arms allow then let it fall, bringing a moment of coolness with its descent. They spit up into the blackness, and the moisture returns to their faces like rain.

"A B C D," Willie says, and Jonathan joins in, "E F G H I J K L M N O... " They stop, giggling loudly, each having failed to trick the other, then finish in unison, "Pee!"

The following day, Joe and Teddy will scold them for swearing in bed, but for now, they are conquerors of sorts, having defeated their own inhibitions through united effort. They challenge each other to find a rhyme for bell, but neither has the courage to transgress that far.

Jonathan rolls over on his side, trying to fall asleep but has no success. His pillow is too hot; it burns his

79

cheek. He turns the pillow over until that side becomes too hot, then turns it again; turns his head to try the other cheek. His head becomes so dense with heaviness, so huge and unmanageable that he cannot move it. A great weight presses down on him; his brain takes on the consistency of water. He can no longer think clearly, does not want to think; the heaviness, the dizziness, now spinning and falling, swirling darkness rushing into a vacuum.

They awaken at the same instant. Early morning bolts of lightning brighten the sky and enter the window to frighten them. Distant thunder rolls in over the woods, growing from faint rumblings to loud crashes. Then the rain comes banging against the roof and leaking through onto them. They get up to push the bed to a dry spot near the back wall, then have to move a second time when water comes dripping down from another hole. They finally find a dry spot, but by the time the sun rises, the bed is soaking wet anyway, though, as usual, it is of their own combined doing.

Working with Father

"Come with me," Father says. "I want you to help me."

Jonathan moans. He slams his comic book down and whines, "Can't Willie do it? He likes to work."

"No! Willie can't do it. I told you to. Come on. It won't take long."

They leave the house and go past Grandma's to the shed where there is some kind of motor lying on the ground. It looks and smells greasy, and he feels certain he will be forced to put his hands on it.

Kneeling beside the motor, Father raises it from the horizontal to the vertical, then balances it between his hands. "Now, I want you to hold it like this so I can work on it."

Jonathan grimaces. He cannot remember a time when Father has demanded his help and really needed it; everytime it is something which could be done by one person. "Can't you lean it against something?"

Father glares icily at him. "I said hold it. And you'd better not let it fall."

Jonathan exhales a deep breath of disgust but does as he is told. The sun beats mercilessly down as long minutes tick off. Father's movements cause the motor to jerk back and forth, creating further annoyance. To make matters worse, while he is squatting, head bowed in misery and eyes downcast, he notices that the seam in the crotch of his jeans has come apart.

"All right," Father says after minutes which have seemed like hours, "You can let go now."

He lets go, then, with his finger, examines the rip in his pants. Vaguely aware of the motor falling softly back to its original position, he wonders if the tear is bad enough to bring to Mother's attention. It is likely that no one can see it and getting it fixed might cause some inconvenience. He spreads the rip apart, testing it. The rest of the seam holds fast. He hears Father clear his throat and looks up to find the man's dark eyes full of something more than sternness, more like the loathing one has for a disgusting insect.

"People who do that get put in the crazy house."

Jonathan squints in perplexity, wondering what terrible thing he has done, but shrugs his shoulders and asks, "Can I go now?"

The Rookie

Jonathan's first game before spectators is played in front of an admiring crowd consisting of Grandma seated on her porch, Mother, Sis, Cousin Annie, and Aunt Jane. He wishes that Father was there to see it instead of working the swing shift.

He is given the honor of leading off. With Aunt Jane nearby, he steps up to the bare patch of ground which is home plate and takes his stance. Joe crouches toward him, ball in hand. The fielders are amused, yelling encouragement. Aunt Jane claps her hands as her booming voice orders him to hit the ball. He wishes that she would be quiet; this is a boy's game.

Joe lobs the ball toward the plate. Jonathan steps into the pitch and, at the same instant, Aunt Jane yells, "Swing!". The swing has already started; it is too late to stop it as he would like to in order to show his independence; a slight uppercut aimed at the center of the arcing ball. The bat makes contact and the ball goes looping off to the side. "Run!" Aunt Jane yells, laughing proudly for her darling.

"Shut up!" he thinks; "It's a foul ball," but he obediently sprints toward first base. Joe takes off leisurely

83

after the ball, stops to let him pass, then continues on. The first baseman leans casually against the oak tree, arms crossed over his chest and eyes gazing into the orchard across the street. When Jonathan reaches the tree, he spins around then copies the first baseman's pose. He realizes that this is not a legitimate base hit and feels cheated. He carefully avoids Aunt Jane's doting eyes and leans toward second, poised with foot braced against the trunk of first, knowing what he has to do if only she will let him.

Epilogue 5

Little Boy is passing Simon's house. He sees the boy sitting on his porch. Simon is blond-haired and blue-eyed and always has a sweet-shy smile on his face. Little Boy wonders what his cut-off tongue looks like, but Simon never opens his mouth. He never makes a sound. The child is happy now, patting the severed head, rolling it around and around in his lap, gazing fondly down at it.

Thief

Jonathan enters the small store at the top of the hill. A nickel clutched in his hand, he walks to the penny-candy counter and tries to decide what he wants. A man is leaning on the soda cooler, exchanging grown-up wisdom with Casey, the proprietor. Figuring it is best to get the most for his money, Jonathan slides the coin onto the countertop then gazes lustfully at boxes containing jawbreakers, banana candy, nigger babies, root beer barrels, and candy corn. Before he can inform Casey of his desires, the man grins down at him and says, "Come around back here and pick what you want," then steps over to the cash register and resumes his conversation with the other man.

Jonathan goes to the rear of the counter, overwhelmed by the faith which Casey has in him and determined to complete the transaction properly. He kneels on the floor and peers inside. The vast array of candies is a treasure even greater than he had at first thought; the temptation one he has not been properly prepared to challenge. He cannot make up his mind but fingers the candy almost blindly until he accumulates a nickel's worth. It is here that his body begins to tremble and his mind goes numb. Neither of the men is paying him any attention. He cannot push himself away from the counter because there is so much more still in it that he really wants. Certain that Casey will not miss them, he takes a jawbreaker, two extra root beer barrels, then, with sweat forming on his brow and a constriction in his chest, he hurriedly grabs two balloons then leaps to his feet before more damage can be done.

The men are still talking, ignoring him as he makes his escape on unsteady legs. Jonathan feels an urge to run, but, with a mighty effort of will, he walks at a normal pace. Every few steps he glances back over his shoulder to see if he is being followed. He shoves a root beer barrel into his mouth and sucks on it. The candy tastes good, though he thinks it shouldn't.

The Bad Tooth

After a day of holding a bottle of warm water to his cheek, waiting for Father to come home from work, Jonathan found himself on the way to the dentist's office to have a tooth pulled, with inklings of the unknown torturing his mind. Then, with Mother and Father at his side, he was laid out in a strange chair and told that everything was okay.

"Do you have to go to the bathroom?" Father asked.

Jonathan shook his head, wanting to get the pain over with as quickly as possible.

The dentist brought a kind of mask up from someplace and slid it over the boy's mouth and nose. "Close your eyes," the man said, "and start counting as high as you can. This won't hurt. You'll just fall asleep, and when you wake up, it'll be all over."

"What will be all over?" Jonathan wondered but couldn't ask. He also wanted to inform everyone there that yes, he did have to go to the bathroom. Something smelled peculiar as he breathed in, counting silently almost into blackness, fearing that he would awaken with wet pants and embarrass himself and his parents.

He reached up and shoved the mask aside. "I don't feel good."

The dentist droned a mild scolding with words which Jonathan couldn't understand, then slid the mask back into place.

Darkness swept in, holding spider webs. Creatures stirred somewhere beyond the reach of his mind but he knew they were there, communicating with each other and plotting against him. Then the darkness was gone, turned to gray and eventually light with commiseration.

The bloated sensation in his stomach remained as they drove homeward, complicated by carsickness and an overall listlessness. They stopped short of the bridge so he could lean out through the door and vomit, then completed the journey in an air of gloom.

The White Whip

During Cousin John's visit, there was a serious accident. It happened on a moonless, overcast night while the children were playing cowboys. Jonathan decided that he would be the hero, The Black Whip, patterning himself after his favorite movie character, although he had only a length of white string tied to a stick and had to alter his name because of that.

He was chasing the bad guys around to the rear of Grandma's house and through the darkness of her garden, snapping the whip at their backs. Once, in the pitch-black of the garden, he not only lost sight of the others but could not see the ground. He was tripped by a potato plant and went down onto the bare earth. As he fell, he reached out to soften his landing, still clutching the whip handle in his hand.

The stick end punctured his cheek, poking through so swiftly that the pain did not immediately register. For a few seconds, he lay still, unaware of what had happened. Then the pain came and with it a warm bubbling fluid which filled his mouth. He leaped to his feet but was afraid to move. He slapped his hand to his cheek and felt the warm liquid flow across his fingers.

"Mommy! Mommy!"

Jonathan finally found the strength to move. He ran past the questions and groping fingers of he didn't know who, along the side of Grandma's house to the lit driveway in front of the porch where someone was bound to save him. A crowd gathered around the bawling child who was spitting frothy blood and complaining that his cheek hurt. Aunt Jane came running from the house, followed by Cousin John. Jonathan was led along the path to his house, crying silently now and trying to be brave.

Inside, Mother assessed the damage, explained that the stick had gone completely through his cheek into his mouth, and tried to stem the flow of blood. "Someone had better take him to the doctor," she said.

Father was working the swing shift and was unavailable, but Cousin John volunteered to do the favor. Man and boy climbed into the car and started the five-mile trip to the doctor's office.

"Don't worry," Cousin John said, smiling solicitously, "you're going to be okay." When Jonathan merely stared blankly back at him, he added, "The doctor will fix you up as good as new."

The tears had dried and the sharp pain had been reduced to a dull ache. This state lasted only as long as he kept his mouth shut; when he tried to open it, the pain returned. This condition was suitable to him since he could find no reason to open his mouth. He had never been alone with an adult before like this, except for his parents, and he had never been in a position where it was necessary to talk to one unless it was to answer a question or respond to a demand. Therefore, he said nothing and merely shook his head at the kindly though one-sided conversation.

"Does it still hurt?" Cousin John asked.

Jonathan nodded, holding a damp washcloth to his cheek to keep the blood from flowing again. He could tell from the calm eyes and soft voice that this near-stranger liked him, and this served to increase his determination to be brave.

Doctor James was waiting in his office when they arrived. Cousin John apologized for the inconvenience,

91

but the doctor shrugged it off. "Let's take a look at the little fellow," he said, then examined the cheek with a humming cheerfulness, as though such tragedies were commonplace to him and no cause for upset nerves.

Jonathan sat still on the examining table and followed the instructions which were given to him without complaint or comprehension. As the doctor patted and fumbled at his cheek, there was no pain. This seemed surprising. When the doctor finished, he patted Jonathan on the head then helped him to the floor, complimenting him for his bravery and patience.

Back in the car, he felt warm from the doctor's admiration and Cousin John's good-natured concern. He lifted a hand to his cheek and, for the first time, realized that it had been bandaged. He suddenly felt eager to get home so the others could see what had been done to him, so they all could admire his bravery.

Summer Scenes

Jonathan sits at the sewing machine, his foot pumping the treadle in a steady rhythm. The needle rises and falls through a piece of scrap cloth, the thread forming an irregular pattern as he tries to master the art of machine sewing. He learns to thread the needle and to change bobbins, much to the disinterest of Mother who is otherwise occupied.

Later, alone in his room with a pair of scissors and an old blanket, he clips out the shape of a pair of pants, once for the front and again for the back. Then, using large stitches, he sews the two pieces together and slips into them. He wears his homemade trousers all that afternoon and into the evening, playing in the yard with imaginary friends until Willie comes home.

But his brother's head shakes with disgust at the inept handiwork. "You look stupid in that," he says. When they enter the house, Willie informs Mother that Jonathan is an embarrassment to the family and should not be let out looking that way.

"Don't make fun of him," Mother replies. "He made those pants all by himself."

"It looks like it."

93

Although Jonathan appreciates Mother's support, he hurries up the stairs to his room and changes back into his regular pants. Sometime during the following days, the new pants disappear without his knowing or caring.

Relatives arrived from north and south for the clambake. Tables had been set up on the lawn for a wide variety of foods and condiments. People wove in and out between each other, beer in one hand and hot-buttered corn in the other, exchanging pleasantries and bits of wisdom.

Horseshoe stakes were pounded into the ground. The men occupied themselves at that sport while the women gathered near Grandma's front porch, though Mother busied herself in her own kitchen. Boys stood around watching the men pitch horseshoes. Most of the girls stayed with the women.

Cousin Lilly, aged three and enamored of Jonathan, followed him into the house and up the stairs to his bedroom where she got tossed onto his bed again and again. Each time he threw her, she laughed hysterically, bouncing on the mattress then leaping back to the floor begging to be picked up and thrown again. And, each time he threw her, Jonathan watched her dress slide up and her legs spread apart, hoping for a glimpse of her secret parts, but there was only the white of her panties. When he finally said he was tired of the game, she followed him back down the stairs, still laughing and demanding his attention. Mother smiled as they went by, believing it had all been innocent fun.

Early in the evening, chairs were brought out to the lawn and the remaining relatives sat while they drank their beer. Jonathan sat on one of the folding chairs, watching Lilly's baby sister romp barefooted through the grass. She wore diapers that sagged, exposing much of her anatomy below the navel, and as he watched, he held a running wish that the diapers would fall and that he would see what he so desperately wanted to see, but, almost by magic it seemed, the diapers stayed where they were meant to stay.

After dark, the final remaining male relatives gathered in Father's living room. They discussed the war and the strategy needed to end it, the abuses by management of labor and all the scheming that went on in company offices. There were derogatory tales about niggers, wops, polacks, and Jews; there was talk about car engines, tractors, horses, buying cheap, the need to be clever and to outwit all the scoundrels of the world, the eternal conflict between good and evil, the adversities of life and how courage and determination could overcome them if luck was on one's side; a listing of the sick and the dead and of good hunting dogs and fishing lures; discussions of what appeared to be secret knowledge and the intricate and often perverse workings of mankind. In all of this, Jonathan found great wisdom. He wondered if he would ever possess even a tiny fraction of that wisdom; doubted if this was possible; realized that he simply did not have the capacity.

As he sat listening, a tension fell upon him, a tightening of the jaw muscles. He tried to relax, couldn't, massaged his jaw, yawned his mouth wide-open and worked the jaw back and forth and up and down, becoming more and more aware of himself as the voices faded away in the darkness of the room, until faces were merely black shadows which moved soundlessly like the bogeyman, until it all became focused on the angry face of Father bent toward him and growling, "I think you'd better go up to bed."

Jonathan knew he had been embarrassing Father, that, because of this, he should also be embarrassed, and he was. He leaped to his feet and ran upstairs to his room, undressed for bed, slipped between the sheets and quietly cried himself to sleep.

Mother is leaning against the Kalamazoo stove, talking to Father who has just entered the room. Father walks over to her, lays his hand on her shoulder, then leans forward slightly to give her a peck on the cheek. Jonathan is stunned by this unusual display of passion and wonders if it is proper.

She is standing at the kitchen stove, ladling hot

95

tomatoes into canning jars. Her round body is dark in the dim light as she mops sweat from her brow. The smell of stewed tomatoes fills the air; not exactly pleasant but at least reassuring. Up close, he inhales an odor that is even more pungent; from beneath the wrinkled dress and body sweat comes the smell of soup bones, rabbit guts, salt pork and sauerkraut, house dust and mop water, dog messes, musty bureaus, fish heads, garbage pails and bread dough, old corsets and ancient wisdom, the mystery of motherhood.

Cousin Bob, Willie, and Jonathan are playing near the creek. They charge through ferns, investigate a tree with messages and names carved in its bark, explore winding cow trails and the island below round-rock. A fish leaps from the water and Cousin Bob exclaims, "What the hell!"

"What the hell!" Willie parrots.

"God damn!" Cousin Bob says.

"God damn!" Willie says.

Both boys laugh, but Jonathan is offended. He walks away from the two sinners and climbs the hill to home. He finds Aunt Jane visiting in the living room and sternly informs her, "Bobby and Willie are down by the creek, swearing."

Instead of praising him, Aunt Jane laughs then continues her conversation with Mother. Noticing his dismay, however, she pats him on the head then offers her lips for a kiss. He grimaces inside himself but kisses her, uncertain whether it is meant to be a reward or punishment.

Oliver is drunk and sputtering, trying to get into the house while Father tries to explain why he can't come in. The man had come to Father, who is president of the local papermakers' union, to seek help in settling a grievance. He has a cleft palate and is barely understandable when he speaks; now liquor has slurred it into almost complete incomprehensibility.

"Look," Father says with growing annoyance, "you're drunk. I don't want you in my house."

"Listen to me," Oliver complains, sticking a leg through the narrow opening, "I need your help. They want to fire me." There is so much pain in that voice that Jonathan thinks the man is about to cry. Oliver swears, not in anger but in desperation.

"See me at work tomorrow," Father says coldly, "when you're sober." He pushes and, when the man staggers backwards, slams the door shut.

From outside, the voice bawls on incoherently. Only that terrible pain is recognizable.

Jonathan wishes that Father would let the man come in. He knows that Oliver is not bad, but he also knows that Father is not trying to be unkind.

He is standing in the kitchen in his underwear, when, through the open door, he spies Aunt Jane walking through the darkness along the path from Grandma's house toward his. She climbs the rotting stairs and crosses the shaky porch, then enters the kitchen. She stops when she sees him, shakes her head with a "tsk! tsk!", then scolds him: "You shouldn't let me see you in your underwear." But she smiles, so Jonathan knows she isn't really angry.

For some reason he doesn't try to comprehend, he is not embarrassed; he is even happy that she has seen him like this, and in some mysterious way, he finds it thrilling.

Mother is sitting at the dining room table, writing out a shopping list. Her pocketbook is near her hand for ready reference, and when he sees it, he says, "Mommy, can I have a nickel for gum?"

"No!" she says firmly, continuing to concentrate on the list without so much as a glance in his direction.

"Please?"

"I said no! Now leave me alone!"

"Please, Mommy. Just a nickel. I won't ask again. I promise."

She takes a deep breath but still refuses to look at him.

Jonathan remembers rehearsing what he would say,

and how he would say it, if he was ever kidnapped. In his softest, nicest voice, he would plead with the kidnapper not to kill him; he would even make his eyes soft and nice so the kidnapper could tell what a good boy he is, and the kidnapper being, like all adults, a good person deep inside, he would be forced by his conscience to let Jonathan go. In that frame of mind, he makes himself go soft all over, sends his spirit out through his blue eyes to gently touch Mother, and half-whispers, "Mommy, please?"

Once again she says no, without looking in his direction, but he can tell, from some subtle collapse in part of her demeanor, that she is aware of more than his physical presence.

For what he decides will be his last attempt, he speaks once more, this time allowing a slight tremolo in his breathy voice, as though throwing a hint that he might be on the verge of tears; "Please, Mommy. I never get anything." Then, seeing her hand rise to cover her eyes as she leans forward, sighing, he adds, "Just a nickel?"

She reaches into the pocketbook, removes a nickel and slams it down on the table. "Now get out of here and leave me alone!"

Jonathan picks the coin up. "Thank you," he says, his voice still soft and full of love. He leaves the house, slides onto the seat of his bike, and heads for the store.

For hours, Jonathan lies tossing and turning in the hot, humid air, but as midnight deepens into morning, his awareness evaporates into blackness. Morning thickens, darkens to a heavy peacefulness which presses like a physical weight upon his chest. He is sinking under this weight, grasping for stars which are not there or any kind of fingerhold which will allow him to pull his soul back up where it should be, above and beyond this oppressive, stifling suffocation, but he is unaware of all this turmoil until a loud explosion awakens him.

He is lying on his back, his body so still it might be dead. His mind functions feebly, moving sluggishly from sleep to whatever state he has arrived at, trying to determine from where the explosion had come. He gradually reaches the conclusion that it had come from his chest.

As he thinks of his chest, he notices that he is not breathing and when he tries to breathe discovers that he is unable to do so. This worries him. Then, when he tries to move his arms, he finds that he cannot do this either. Now, unable to move or breathe, he becomes terrified, wanting to cry out to Willie for help but unable to make a sound. He is afraid he will die but knows that if he can move just one finger, it will save him. He summons all his willpower, concentrates all of his energy into his right hand, strains with all his might, and after moments of near panic, the hand moves, the spell is broken and he is once more able to breathe. He rolls over onto his side, gasping, afraid to return to sleep. There are tears of exertion in his eyes. He wants to reach out and awaken Willie, to tell him what has happened and to share his terror with him, but doesn't.

Epilogue 6

A detective is investigating the murders. He enters a large room where many people are gathered. A man bumps into him then hurries away without apologizing. The fleeing man is the murderer, but the detective does not know this. Instead, he pushes through the crowd toward two men who are fighting savagely across the room. He wants to find out why they are fighting. Another thing the detective does not know is that one of these men was a victim of the murderer.

The fighting men vanish and the detective sits down on a chair. A woman looks at him, gaining his attention. She throws something. At least he thinks she is the one. Then confusion sets in and he thinks it might have come from the fleeing man. It is small and white, possibly a piece of chalk. He catches it. He knows it is a clue but knows nothing more than this.

Third Grade

There is a new setup in school this year: First, second, and third grades are in one room and fourth, fifth, and sixth in another. The room previously used as a first and second grade room is now used as an auditorium, mostly for playing badminton on rainy days and for school assemblies. The upper floor of the firehouse, once used as an auditorium, had been destroyed by fire, including the beautiful red stage curtains. Shale slates from the roof are still scattered over the ground, and children, intrigued by the smooth, flat shapes, continually search for them and pick them up, as they would Indian arrowheads, but they do not know quite what to do with them.

Jonathan has a new friend. Eddie, along with brother Mike and sister Grace, has moved from the city to live temporarily with an uncle. Eddie's behavior is slightly eccentric but in a decent sort of way. He brags about possessing knowledge and skills which are beyond those of the other boys, having experiences they are deprived of due to their location in the sticks, but Jonathan shrugs this off as nothing more than city-talk. Actually, he judges Eddie's talents to be somewhat inferior to his own and to his classmates, but this bears no importance to their relationship since the boy is a true and loyal friend.

Eddie is quickly tested by Frankie and James one recess when they confront him before the other children, Frankie grabbing the newcomer's shirtfront and shoving him against a wall, James by his side looking menacingly on, warning him that they run the schoolyard and if he thinks otherwise they can settle the matter there and then. While Jonathan mutely watches with the others, though debating within himself if it is worth the effort to get involved, trembling Eddie acquiesces. Jonathan is unable to forgive himself for his indecisiveness, or cowardice, whichever it has been, but he is convinced that confrontation at this time will only lead to future confrontations, and he has grown tired of rising to meet the bullies' challenges, especially since he is the only one with enough daring to fight back. There is still an occasional wrestling match with Frankie or some other aggressive boy, matches which Jonathan wins because of superior body control and determination, but he sees himself growing into the image of his bad-tempered brothers and bringing on himself a reputation among the townspeople which he does not want, and he fervently hopes that the fighting will someday stop.

He and Eddie play together on the schoolground and at each other's house, and they swim together at the sandbar north of the bridge. Early in the fall, they explore the woods, setting fires in the openings of rabbit holes then extinguishing them, until one fire spreads out of control into a large circle and Jonathan runs up the hill for help and the fire department is summoned. Firemen, and a crowd, arrive to surround and douse the flames. When Jonathan explains how the fire had started and how Eddie had begged him not to tell anyone because they would get in trouble, Aunt Jane declares him a hero then gives his friend a severe tongue-lashing.

Jonathan and Willie are hired by the neighboring farmer to pick up drops in his apple orchard at 10¢ a crate. James is also hired, but he and Jonathan tire of the job after filling one crate each. They begin eating

102

the apples, then throwing them, then running with out-stretched arms, rat-a-tat-tatting like machine guns and humming like airplane engines, to drop bombs on Japs and on Hitler. By the end of the workday, they have fill-ed three crates each to Willie's 33.

Mornings before school are troublesome times, mo-ments of distress and confusion. He misplaces articles of clothing, is unable to find them quickly enough to suit Mother or the older children, and in his haste to find them becomes panicked by the castigations of Teddy, Sis, Willie, and Mother—mostly Mother. She scolds loud-ly and angrily as he races from room to room in circles around the bottom floor, reminding him of his useless-ness, incompetence, dumbness, of how grating on the nerves he is and how she wishes he was forever out of her sight, until his eyes are so filled with tears that he cannot see, and still no one moves to help him. Finally, he locates the item right where he had left it; the first place he had looked. He leaves the house, Mother letting him know how happy she is to see him go, to trail, ig-nored as though he doesn't exist, the others up the long hard road to school.

In school, his reading skills win high grades but his penmanship is atrocious. In spelling, he achieves a score of 86, or a grade equivalency of 5.5 and two years in advance of his age. His worst score is a 70 in arithmetic problems, but this is still one grade and one month ahead of himself. On the playground, he more often than not makes contact with the pitched ball and many times is able to punch it through the infield. Frankie, however, often reaches the tennis court on the fly, an act of pow-er so prodigious it is beyond any of the other boys' wild-est dreams.

This school year holds some early excitement when the furnace malfunctions and threatens to explode. The students are evacuated in an orderly fashion, just the way they had been drilled, but Teddy stays behind to help bring the furnace back under control and becomes an instant, though brief, hero. A short time later, in the semi-darkness of the auditorium, Teddy is yanked from his seat by a teacher, takes a swing at her, and is suspended.

At home, after finishing his homework at night, Jonathan paints pictures of the sun setting through the trees beyond Grandma's house, their branches spread along the horizon like spider webs. The darkness brings a chill of separation, of distance from his parents who view his artwork with disguised pleasure, suggesting that he put as much effort into doing his chores. Instead, his own world shrinking closer and closer to himself and more distant from the others, he settles at the table into the late hours, drawing P-40s, bombers, tanks, and cars. With crayons, he creates winter scenes of snowmen, angels, and Jesus in the manger, eyeing his own sad reflection in the night-black windows, bitter and angry because Joe, Teddy, Sis, and Willie are having fun in town and he is not allowed to venture away from home.

The Birthday Party

As he was about to leave for the party, Jonathan asked if he was supposed to take a present. Mother sighed, looked about for something appropriate, and spotted an old box containing a jigsaw puzzle. She wrapped it, handed it to him, and sent him on his way.

Jonathan pedalled his bike up the street, past the farm and almost to the town proper. He turned left up a short, dead-end lane to James's house. Embarrassed by his cheap gift, hoping that none of the pieces were missing just in case someone decided to assemble it, he handed it to the boy as he was greeted at the door.

The party took place on the rear lawn, where games were played and ice cream and cake were served. James's mother directed the activity. Jonathan told her he was having a great time and wished they could have a party every day. She smiled, said that he was talking too fast and she couldn't understand him; would he please repeat himself.

"Isaidthisisfun. Iwishwecoulddoiteveryday."

"Honey, you'll have to slow down."

He tried again, then once more, but couldn't say it slowly enough for her to understand. "Never mind," he said, shrugging his shoulders.

Later, as he was leaving, James thanked him for the present. Jonathan searched for a note of insincerity in the voice but could find none. He looked at the face, at the blue eyes, and saw only honesty and was pleased.

Riding home in the darkness, along the stretch of road between the farm and his house, he sang happily as he thought of the party. There were no streetlights here and he had to let the front tire feel its way on the blacktop. As though it was a distant star, the light from the living room window guided his direction.

Then, as it always seemed to happen when he was riding in the dark in that area, two cars approached from opposite directions. He steered off the road into the weeds by the ditch. The oncoming headlights blinded him but he continued on, knowing that he was probably safe as long as the bike kept wobbling over the rough ground. The cars passed each other directly beside him, one only a couple of feet away.

Safely at home, he ran to tell Mother of the party as she sat knitting, but she merely gave a disinterested shrug of the shoulders and said, "That's nice."

"Eagles!"

One fine fall day found Cousin Bob, Willie, and Jonathan quietly fishing at creekside. Suddenly, the serenity was broken by a burst of rapid screeching sounds which pierced the woods from a distance. The cries were shrill and deadly, and Jonathan knew instinctively what they were coming from. Leaping to his feet, he yelled, "Eagles!" At any moment, he expected to see their terrifying shapes come crashing down through the treetops, razor-sharp claws reaching out to rip his eyes from their sockets.

The others were on their feet, too, already moving in the direction of the sounds and about to leave him behind. "Eagles, nothing!" Cousin Bob said in passing. "That's Brownie!"

Jonathan ran to keep up with them as they pushed through a patch of ferns, coming out close to a barbed-wire fence which marked their property line. There, in the underbrush, they found the dog, her paw caught in the jaws of a trap. Cousin Bob and Willie rushed to her side and began to fumble with the trap. Jonathan turned and ran. With Brownie's yelps stabbing at his back, he raced up the hill, took the path above the stream's steep clay bank, ducked through the fence then scrambled up the dump hill, and there found Father raking leaves.

"Daddy! Daddy!" he yelled on the run, then stopped directly in front of the man.

Father looked at him with mild curiosity. "What's the trouble?"

Jonathan stood gasping, unable to get the words out at first, his eyes seeing Father distorted by a thick lens of tears. Then he said, "Browniegotherfootcaughtina-trapandcan'tgetitout!"

"What?" Father said, annoyed.

"Browniegotherfootcaughtinatrapandcan'tgetitout!"

"Wait! Wait! Slow down so I can understand you."

"Brownie— " The sentence built in his chest, wanting to blow him apart, but he couldn't speak it. He managed, "Downbythecreek—," then started sobbing.

Father looked away, sighed, then slowly walked over to the shed and placed the rake inside. By the time he returned, Cousin Bob appeared at the top of the hill, Brownie in his arms and Willie behind him.

The dog was whimpering, her paw bloody but not seriously injured. Jonathan hugged and petted her, angry with himself for his incompetence and uselessness, for having fallen apart at just the moment she had needed him. He had proved himself weak, a failure, and, had it not been for the bigger boys, Brownie might have died because of him.

The Headless Horseman

One Saturday morning, Willie and Jonathan walk eastward along the gravel road south of their property to fish in the pond near their uncle's farmhouse. Ahead is a deep ravine where the road dips through a wooded area. Squinting from the sun directly ahead of them, they notice something moving near the ridge, cutting across their path. Perhaps it is only a shadow sweeping through the dust, but it is gray and has four legs, looking very much like a horse, on its back a rider hunched over, clinging to the reins, the man's head either lost in the hanging dust motes or simply not there.

Halloween

Early in the evening, the children start up the road toward town. Anxious to get there, Jonathan runs ahead of the others, past the neighbor's farmhouse and some woodland, then to a house belonging to one of the farmer's two sons.

Two figures emerge from the darkness so suddenly that he is unable to resist when grabbed and lifted onto their shoulders. The men hold him so he cannot struggle, and one says to the other, "Let's take him inside. We'll lay him on the table and pull his pants down."

Jonathan tries to kick but his legs are held too tightly. He thinks about yelling for help but can hear his brothers and sister talking near the farmhouse and is sure they will see his abduction and come to his rescue; yet their voices go steadily on. Then, before fear has a chance to truly grip him, and just as suddenly as he has been grabbed, he finds himself released and standing alone beside the road. A door slams shut and he is left in a vacuum of ringing silence. He trots back to his protectors but does not tell them of the incident; it had been too strange and confusing to put into words.

Up the street, they spot flames in the field far off

to their left in the high grass behind home plate of the ball diamond. A large sleigh belonging to the Jewish grocer is on fire. They walk by, barely commenting on the sight, but Jonathan runs inside the store to inform the owner. The old man is not there; only his son who greets Jonathan's story with amused skepticism.

Having performed his duty, Jonathan leaves the store to find Sis and Willie waiting for him, Joe and Teddy having gone off to do mischief with the town's older boys. The three of them walk east past the schoolhouse road, stopping with their bags at houses along the way, then return to the main street to head back south toward home, stopping for more popcorn, apples, cider, and candy.

They reach home with their bags full, yet complaining about the Thompsons, a young couple who had turned off their houselights and pretended they weren't home.

The Accident

Sitting at his desk, Jonathan raises his hand to go to the bathroom. His mind has escaped from his skull and is already racing down the stairs to the basement, but it rushes past the boys' room, past the furnace, to the other end of the building where it seeps through the door of the girls' room. Inside his head stands a faceless adult. Jonathan asks why boys aren't allowed in the girls' room—what is that horrible secret they must keep from him. There is no reply to the question. His imagination captures several faceless girls milling about in the bathroom; places one of them on a toilet bowl, but it is dark in there and her dress is down over the important part. He cannot lift the dress. The cement floor is cold and menacing, so he flees.

Now he is sitting on the bowl, having relieved himself. He reaches down between his legs to squeeze his bladder. It is empty and his two kidneys float freely inside. By the end of the day, the bladder feels full again. Once outside in the cold, his need becomes more urgent. He runs ahead of the other children, out to the slick road then down to the post office on the corner. He hurries inside and up to the window.

"Can I please have our mail?"

The postmaster smiles and says, "Just a minute, Jonathan. I have to finish up here."

The postmaster is also his godmother, a Sunday school teacher, church organist and organizer, Mother's cousin; and for these and other reasons, he thinks it would be improper to tell her to hurry. Instead, he does a dance of desperation while she patiently occupies herself, unseen, behind the wall of combination boxes.

"Hurry up! Please!" he screams inside his head, feeling pressure building against his dam of nerves. The structure begins to crack, then crumbles to ruin and water rushes through to flood his pants. It drips into a growing circle upon the wooden floor, and still there is no sign of the postmaster.

Jonathan flees through the door. There is no one on the street, but he is afraid he might meet someone on the way home. He runs past the Jewish grocery store and dives into a huge snowbank just beyond it, rolling over and over until his entire pants are soaked and the accident unnoticeable.

At home, Mother scolds him about his wet clothes, wonders aloud how he could have gotten them that way, then tells him to change into something dry. He happily obeys.

The Barber

Mr. Foxx is an old man with white hair. For small children, he places a padded board across the arms of the barber chair to bring their heads up to a workable height. He huffs and puffs as he moves his fat body, wrestling the child's head into a proper position for clipping. There is no conversation, only an occasional, "Now hold it steady," or, "What in the world is all this junk in your hair?"

Jonathan squints at the wall mirror, thinking. "Hair tonic." Then, remembering, he adds, "And shampoo."

Mr. Foxx makes a funny sound, then asks, "Why did you put shampoo in your hair?"

"So I could comb it." Jonathan does not like Mr. Foxx's peevish attitude. Neither does he like the constant twisting and tilting of his head, the unforgiving fingers pressing into his cheek and skull, but, most of all, he despises the baby-seat and hopes Mr. Foxx will soon realize he has outgrown it.

At the end comes a dusting with powder, a fine trimming, then the only good part, the rubbing-in of a cool, aromatic tonic and the combing of his hair to a damp, slick mat with a high wave in front. He hopes others will have a chance to see the finished result and offer admiring comments before the winter wind makes a mess of it.

And now that the tribulation is over, the barber shop takes on a friendlier atmosphere: The bottles of cologne and cans of powder, various colored liquids he can't identify, shaving mugs and soap and the straight razor with its strop hanging down from the shelf, even the clock and wall calendar add textures of their own, the manly smells soothe rather than test his sensibility. The hairy floor is there to remind him of his special kinship with other males of the community; fronting the side wall, the candy counter with its temptations and the cash register reminding him not only of his obligation but of the sense of equality awarded by it.

He smiles as Mr. Foxx removes the sheet then slaps off the loose hair which had accumulated beneath it and helps him back to the floor. As he slips into his coat, preparing to leave, the man asks him, "How would you like to do me a favor?"

Jonathan nods his head, smiling. He wonders what kind of favor he could possibly do for anyone but replies, "Okay!"

"Could you find me a Christmas tree? One about this big?" He holds his hand out at waist level.

"Yup!"

"I'll pay you."

Jonathan hurries home, amazed at his good fortune, pleased not only to be helping someone but to also be paid for it. He finds Father's hatchet in the shed, then descends the hill into the woods. The snow is deep, making the going slow and difficult. It is piled high on pine branches, often tumbling off upon him. He plows a two-legged path across animal tracks with one set which he knows belongs to a long-gone deer. Down in the valley of the stream, he crosses at a series of miniature waterfalls, around to the side of the cliff, then a steep climb, pulling himself up to where he knows there is a perfect tree.

It is on the steepest part of the slope, alone in a clearing atop an outcropping of shale. He cannot brace himself and so slides down with each whack of the hatchet, but after a dozen or so blows, he is through and the tree is his. Jonathan drags it up to the top of the hill, past the cliff to the northern end of the plateau, through the fence near James's house and down the lane to the street, then up that and down the hill to the barber shop.

Inside, Mr. Foxx examines the Christmas tree carefully. "Very nice," he admits. He takes it into a rear room then returns to slip behind the candy counter. "Come here," he says. "Pick whichever one you want."

Jonathan goes to the counter, believing there must be more to "pay" than this, hoping that Mr. Foxx intends it as only a beginning.

"That," he says, pointing at a 10¢ Almond Joy. He thanks Mr. Foxx when the man slides the candy bar over to him.

"Thank you for the lovely tree," Mr. Foxx says. "You can go now."

Jonathan walks slowly to the door, hoping the barber will realize his mistake and call him back, but he is allowed to leave with no further compensation. Outside, he thinks he feels angry at Mr. Foxx for cheating him but isn't quite sure. He wonders if it is just another one of his own dumb mistakes; if he had misunderstood the proposition and has only himself to blame.

Bathtime

Baths rarely occur during the summer, since the boys are in the water much of the time anyway. In the cold of late autumn, winter, and early spring, baths take place more frequently, sometimes as often as twice a month.

Water is heated on the kitchen stove in large pans or in the tub itself. Baths are taken in the room at the bottom of the stairs; Willie first, then Jonathan.

"Did you pee in the water?" Jonathan asks as he climbs in and Willie takes the towel to dry himself.

Willie nods his head.

Jonathan pees, too, then shares his brother's amusement. It is a secret act that Mother does not know about, and they can giggle together in the knowledge that they have gotten away with something naughty.

His brother dresses, then leaves to go about his business. Jonathan soaps the washcloth, then scrubs his body. He dries himself on the towel and wraps it around his waist, then goes to the dining room to show Mother how clean he is.

She is sitting at the table doing a crossword puzzle but looks away long enough to nod approvingly.

He raises his foot to the rung of the chair, bracing himself on it as he slides the towel up his pale leg. A slight chill strikes from evaporating moisture and from the sense of daring he feels at exposing the limb almost to the point of immodesty. "Mommy, am I clean enough?"

She turns her attention back to the puzzle, again nodding slightly.

Jonathan skips happily back to the bathroom to dress himself.

The Floating Cat

Jonathan is at creekside after the spring floods. An orange-colored cat is floating in the water near his feet. Not much of it shows and he cannot see the eyes. He is afraid that part of the cat might still be inside: its ghost, or demon. If the eyes are open, perhaps that dark spirit could leap inside of Jonathan's head and suck everything out of his brain and turn his blood to dust. "I hope they're closed," he whispers soundlessly.

Some fur is gone from its side. The skin there is gray. The word, "corpse", enters his mind, but he hurriedly rethinks it as, "Poor, dead cat."

He wonders if the legs are down or tucked-up under. If they are not down, the cat might roll over and float face-up. This seems to be a horrible possibility, especially if the eyes are open.

Some force pushes Jonathan down toward the cat. He struggles to keep his balance, shudders at the thought of touching dead skin.

He wonders, also, if the water has become haunted by the cat's ghost. He doesn't exactly pray but does think about God and the cat both at the same time and hopes that will be enough to chase anything bad from the water and make it pure again.

At last he thinks he has seen all he wants to see. He thinks he knows everything he will ever need to know about dead cats. He takes one last look then turns and scampers up the hill to safety.

Wildflowers

Jonathan searches the damp woods for flowers. He picks enough violets for a small bouquet for Mother. As quickly as he can, he climbs the hill to the house, but by the time he gets there they are wilted. Mother accepts them quietly, her face softening in an undecipherable smile. "Thank you," she says, then disappears into the kitchen to do something with the flowers.

Visit to a Dead Girl

Willie and Jonathan walk the length of their orchard, across a winding driveway and toward a powerline tower in the middle of a hay field. Near the tower, there is a small graveyard, the headstones weather-worn and the names and dates now faint. There are holes in the ground at the bases of a couple of stones, and Jonathan wonders if the spirits of the dead can look up through those holes and see him, or, perhaps, these are holes through which their spirits have passed to Heaven.

He stops in front of one grave and stares solemnly down at the sunken earth. A great sadness falls upon him until he is tempted to weep, but the urge passes, leaving him merely numb.

MARY SCHAFER
1861-1873

The stone is cold beneath the blazing sun, just as her bones are cold beneath the hard earth. Her name sends a chill through him as though the letters are etched in ice. He imagines her dark and pretty, braced against an other-worldly darkness in a long-flowing gown, whispering his name over and over.

122

It is a long time before he notices that Willie has been talking to him and is now halfway back across the field, heading homeward. He runs to catch up with his brother and, together, they return home by way of the orchard.

Epilogue 7

The detective is sitting on a stoop. The girl is sitting beside him. They are listening to people talking nearby. A woman says, "That sweet-shy little boy. He weighed only one and a half ounces more than the head when they buried him." He realizes that Simon, too, has been murdered, and this makes him feel very sad. He loved Simon and blames himself for what has happened. He believes that he should have taken the head away from the little boy instead of letting him play with it. But Simon had looked so happy, and he hadn't wanted to make him cry. And thinking about Simon, the detective becomes more and more determined to find the killer.

The coldness of the women depresses him. The tragedy has not upset them; it has merely given them something to talk about to relieve their boredom.

A man gently pushes a child out onto the sidewalk. He is grinning and is obviously fond of the boy, but there is mockery in his voice. "All you have to do is throw a little pickaninny at them. Nobody can get mad at that."

The detective isn't sure if the man is referring to the mysterious sect responsible for the murders or to the larger society which has been horrified by them.

The girl taps him on the shoulder. When he turns his head and looks into her eyes, he discovers that they are darker and more mysterious than ever. Softly, she whispers, "I know a secret," then they both fade away.

In the Garden

It is a beautiful morning at the end of June. Jonathan awakens to the chirping of birds. He dresses, then hurries down the stairs and outside into a bright, invigorating sunlight. Until Willie comes grumpily out the door to play, he bounces a rubber ball off the front of the house.

Before they can start any kind of game, however, Father calls to them from beyond Grandma's house. "I've got a job for you," he says when they get there. He nods toward the garden. "I want you to pull these weeds."

Only a short time ago, Father, Joe, and Teddy had cleared all the trees from the orchard, and in the process, a garden had been worked in. It is immense, running south for at least a hundred feet and half that distance in width.

Jonathan realizes that it will take forever to weed, that it will be a hot, sweaty, miserable job. "Why do we have to do this?" he grumbles after Father has left.

"Never mind," Willie replies. "Let's just get it over with."

"But he never plays with us." Only the day before, he had asked Father to pitch a few in to him, to see what a good hitter he is, but Father had complained about being too busy.

When Willie doesn't reply but begins plucking weeds, Jonathan puffs up his cheeks and blurts, "Boy!", then follows suit in the next row.

The heat is worse than he had thought, the work even more tedious. He continues to complain to Willie, then to himself, as his brother moves far ahead of him, increasing his lead every minute. Before he is halfway down his first row, Willie is on his second, oblivious to the intolerable working conditions. Jonathan's fingers are already sore; his back and neck ache; the scrawny weeds resist his efforts to pull them.

"If you like this so much," he snarls as Willie passes in the opposite direction, "why don't you do the whole thing?"

Willie ignores him, and for a moment, his mind is filled with loathing. But he struggles staunchly onward to the end of the row. Fifteen, twenty, thirty minutes? It is hard to judge passing time when suffering is so severe. One hour? Two?

He notices that Willie is on his third row, and there are perhaps only two rows more to do. It seems that the entire garden does not need weeding, only this particular section. With renewed strength and determination, he moves forward, sending the weeds flying in a blur of constant motion. He starts on the last row, and Willie meets him at the middle.

When they are done, Jonathan asks, "You wanta play ball, now?"

"No!" Willie says sharply. "I'm going swimming."

"Can I go with you?"

"No. I'm going to the sand bar."

"Why can't I go?"

"Ask Mommy."

"You know she won't let me."

Willie says no more. He takes his bathing suit from the house, hops on his bike, and heads up the street.

Jonathan decides he had better disappear too, before Father finds another job for him.

Grace

Jonathan exited the house one morning to find Willie involved in a whispered conversation with Eddie, his older brother Mike, and sister Grace. Willie motioned to him, saying, "Come on, we're going fishing."

He followed them down the hill, but it was not until they had reached the lower pasture fence that he sensed something odd about the situation. Watching as the boys held the fence wires apart for their sister, he realized what the problem was.

He tapped his brother on the arm and asked, "Where's your fishpole?" None of the others had one either.

"We're not going fishing," Willie said.

"Oh," he said as understanding rushed in.

They walked silently through the woods, Jonathan with a growing eagerness to get there.

Grace stopped once, to pee, and the boys gathered around to watch. She pulled her underwear down but did not expose herself. Instead, she squatted with her long plaid dress forming a tent over her legs and urinated in a way which Jonathan found disturbing.

They remained silent even when they reached the

swimming hole. Acting as though it had been agreed on beforehand, Jonathan began removing his clothes, and the others followed his example. Grace stood directly in front of him, only a couple of feet away. He watched her lift the dress over her head, then remove her underwear the same instant he became naked.

But something was terribly wrong. Something about her. Later, he couldn't remember what it was, though it seemed to involve the possibility of an accident, or an operation; an ugly scar. He remembered averting his eyes, then feeling relief when they were in the water. Though they stood silently side by side, he still could not look at her, knowing she must have suffered intense pain and humiliation.

They had been in the water less than a minute when Willie spotted Sis descending the hill. They leaped atop the bank, grabbed their clothes, and ran to a distant clump of bushes to hide and dress.

Jonathan fell asleep beside Willie that night, thinking of Grace and angry at the confusion he had brought on himself. He dreamed about the girl. She was naked, twisting her body in a dance which wasn't nice, as though she was taunting him, sticking her stomach out and shaking her penis so he'd be sure to see it.

On a later day, he asked Eddie if his sister would go swimming with them again, but the boy shook his head. "She isn't like that anymore."

He never saw Grace again but often thought of her. He tried to remember her face but saw only a mist there; yet sometimes it almost came to him: framed by long black hair were the delicate features, more round and less equine than that of her brothers, a serious mouth and soft dark eyes. He knew that she was pretty and that he loved her.

Supper

One of his jobs is to set the table. A green plate for Willie, the color of shaded grass. A red plate for himself; it has the depth and richness of royal robes. The rest of the plates are distributed randomly, the only other constant being Father's place at the head of the table. Spoons and forks to the right, knives to the left. Mother is usually seated beside Father at the oval table, then Sis, Jonathan, Willie, Joe, then Teddy on Father's other side, the older boys' backs to the windowed wall.

Supper is the only time that Father talks to Jonathan, and then only disparagingly; to complain aloud to everyone of his nervous habits, his laziness, his incompetence, even his appetite: "You must have a tapeworm."

Jonathan swallows hard, wondering if such a calamity is possible. He concentrates with all his might to see if he can feel anything slithering around inside him. His imagination finds a long, snakelike creature extended through the corridor of his intestines, an insatiable hunger driving it to rob him of all his food. Jonathan squints at Father but is afraid to ask if he is serious.

The only compliment he remembers is a remark about his fingers. He had been plinking away at a player

130

piano someone had given the family, a mixture of notes played slowly and delicately with no sense of rhythm or melody, and Father had noticed. Or, the comment might have stemmed from his fondling of Brownie immediately thereafter, as he held the dog on his lap, wondering if she might be constructed in a fashion similar to human females. Or, it might have come from something he is unaware of. But, minutes later, as Father sat down to eat, he said to Mother, "You know, Jonathan has good fingers. Nice and gentle. He'd make a good barber."

The conversation usually centers on individuals and classes of people whom Father and the older boys disapprove of: Local drunks, the upper echelon of management in the company he works for, almost all negroes, many Italians, any eccentric, and strangers.

"I don't know why they ever let all these niggers into this country," Father says. "They just take jobs away from white people."

"They're negroes," Sis replies. "And they have just as much right to live here as we do."

Joe bangs his fist down and the table shakes. His round face is red with anger and his dark eyes glare at Sis. "They're niggers!" he says through clenched teeth.

"Why do you call them that? What have they ever done to you?"

"Done to me?" Joe hisses, wishing she was a boy so he could punch him; yet, even though she is a girl, he knows that the subject matter gives him license to abuse the code of ethics. "I hope you never find out what they do. They're nothing but filthy pigs! They're too lazy to work, and they're not fit to live with human beings."

"You think you know everything," Sis says heatedly. "You believe what other people tell you. You don't know how to think for yourself. If you did, you'd understand."

"Jesus Christ! Who the hell do you think you are? I've seen them. I know what they're like."

"All right! All right!" Mother interrupts. "Can't you talk about something else?"

"Oh, so you've seen them. Does that mean you know how they feel, how they're mistreated? Do you think they're worse than the Morgans?" Sis refers to a

131

family living on the opposite end of the village, in a house which is more dilapidated than their own, a family who does not wash very often, does not try to dress nicely or keep their lawn neat, drinks beer to excess, and makes no attempt to be respectable Christians.

Joe is about to stand up and leave the table before he completely loses his temper. Instead, he shoves his chair back and simply glowers at her.

"Babe," Father says soothingly, "you don't know what you're talking about. Just wait till you get out in the world. You'll see."

"That's right," Teddy says. "I wouldn't turn my back on any nigger. The sooner you learn that, the better off you'll be."

"Niggers!" Willie says. "That's all they are."

"You're all so... so... so... " Sis sputters, so overcome by emotion that she is temporarily at a loss for words.

Jonathan twirls a few strands of plain, buttered spaghetti (he refuses to eat it with sauce) onto his fork but does not raise it to his mouth. He watches Sis's desperate eyes as she seeks a way to lay the truth before them. Her face is as pale and injured as the others are red and furious. Jonathan wishes he could come to her aid but he does not know how to argue at such a high level of sophistication; he does not possess their mature wisdom or experience; anything he says would be thrown back at him with that twisted but indisputable logic that older people have, his words met with scorn if they drew any response at all.

"Please. All of you. There's no use to argue. You're all getting upset," Mother says wearily.

"If she'd just listen for once," Joe says.

"It's like talking to a brick wall," Teddy says.

"Who are you to judge them," Sis says. She bursts into tears but does not leave the table.

Joe looks away in disgust, while Teddy resumes eating. After a while, Sis rubs her eyes and looks pleadingly at Father. "What about Lolly? Do you think he's no good?"

Joe curses again but under his breath this time.

"You know I don't mean Lolly," Father says softly. "There's no better man in the whole world than Lolly."

"What do you think about him?" Sis asks Joe.

"There's nothing wrong with him because he knows his place," Joe explains menacingly.

"Oh brother! And what is his place?"

Unbelievably, Joe's face turns even redder. "With other niggers. He don't act uppity like some of them. He sticks with his own kind."

Sis is about to offer a retort, but Father stops her with a wave of the hand. "Enough! We could argue all night." He suddenly turns on Jonathan, drawing attention to his cleaned plate. "There's something wrong with you. You eat too fast."

Jonathan shakes his head. "I don't eat too fast; you just talk too much."

"No I don't."

That is the end of that argument. He doesn't have the power or privilege to continue.

There is a time that he does try to reach out and make his feelings known, but his effort ends in failure. One day, he is made to do more chores, by both Mother and Father, than he thinks proper and neither one listens to his complaints. Joe, Teddy, Willie, and Sis have all spent the day with friends and are planning to spend the evening in town, also, but when he asks for permission to visit Eddie, Father refuses. Jonathan asks him why, explaining that it isn't fair, but Father simply says, "Because I said you can't. That's why."

A volume of angry words builds in his chest, aimed at everyone seated around the table, but he can't get them out. Tears flood his eyes and stream down his cheeks. He takes a deep breath then speaks with much agony in his voice, "I'm treated like a dog around here."

Father finishes chewing his food then calmly replies, "Is that right?"

The anger and frustration grow, wanting to be set free, but he knows he cannot touch anyone with them. They are all calmly eating, as though they hadn't heard him.

He leaps to his feet and runs from the table into

133

the living room, then jumps onto an easy chair and starts bawling. No one comes to him. They all remain seated at the table, engaged in casual conversation as though he had never existed.

Even Sis has dismissed him from her mind; Sis, whose suffering he has always shared, is beyond reach in his hour of need.

Firebug

He has taken a pack of matches from the kitchen and gone up the street with them, with no conscious purpose. Passing the Jewish grocery store, he notices one of the town characters exiting the front door and pedals over to him.

"Hi, Buck," he says brightly, trying to display an air of friendliness.

Buck grunts but otherwise ignores him.

"Would you like to buy some matches for ten cents?" Jonathan holds the pack out for the man's inspection.

"Why should I pay you ten cents when I can get them for nothing?" Buck brushes by him and heads down the street.

Only slightly dismayed by this lesson in business, Jonathan rides his bike past the second grocery store then down the hill. Halfway to the bottom, where the road curves around a large estate, he is struck by inspiration. The lawn, fronted by a supporting wall that he often walks on top of, is the perfect target for the sense of power the matches have given him and for some bad feelings he has brought with him. He does not think about these feelings but sincerely believes that a good fire will burn them away.

Seeing, in his mind, roaring flames consume the lawn, perhaps the big house and the woods behind it, fire trucks rushing to the scene with sirens screaming and people running from every direction, he holds a lit match in a clump of grass. After several seconds, the match fizzles out and he tries another, with the same result, then a third. When no raging inferno results and that match goes out, he shrugs his shoulders in mild disappointment and leaves the scene of the attempted crime.

War's End

Mother received a letter from her brother, Jonathan's Uncle Lou. He had fought in Germany but said he would be home soon, poking his bald head in the door. Mother was outraged by this negative reference to his pate, but Jonathan was amused when he heard her and Aunt Jane discussing the matter. He hoped they would forgive Uncle Lou and that he would be home soon, because he wanted to see this man who had been so often and so favorably discussed during the war.

Meantime, the war with Japan continued, until a day when Cousin Bob, Willie, and he were at the swimming hole and the fire alarm in town began to wail. "The war's over," Cousin Bob announced, and the three boys grabbed their clothes and started up the hill toward home because that seemed to be the proper thing to do.

Fourth Grade

He is now on the second floor with the big kids and considers this no small wonder. There are children, grades 1-3, whom he can feel superior to in a benevolent way, and there is a spiritual equality with the older children, even eighth graders, now that they are housed on the same physical level.

Eddie has moved back to the city, but it is Grace whom he misses most.

His Individual Profile Chart shows him about two years in age and two grades ahead of himself in English and Literature; over one year and one grade in Spelling and Vocabulary; about average in Reading Comprehension, Arithmetic, and Geography; slightly below in History and Civics. His penmanship has barely improved, and his Arithmetic papers are always messy.

He participates in school programs. In one performance before parents in the refurbished firehouse, his part is that of a boy who reads so fast that the teacher makes him say "and" after every word of a story he is reading aloud. This is a true-life situation, the teacher being aware of Jonathan's capability. It is a brilliant comedic performance, he believes, and his only disappointment is that Mother is not in the audience.

One day, he is kept in during recess, although innocent of any wrongdoing. The punishment is the result of a misunderstanding, the teacher believing that Jonathan had whispered to a classmate. He sits at his desk along the wall near a large window in his cub scout uniform, bitter at the injustice, and a tear falls from his cheek onto the paper upon which he is writing, "I will not whisper in class." Amelia, a fifth grader, is sitting in the middle of the room, concentrating on her history book and unaware of his misery.

During the winter, he becomes a protector of girls, defending the screaming victims of snowball attacks by boys who ignore his efforts at reprisal.

In the spring, the class earns money by selling seeds. He is successful because he says, "Yes, ma'am," to ladies and smiles pleasantly. He invites James to ride with him to his old town, where lives, he says, a nice colored man who is sure to buy from them. They pedal their bikes along the stretch of road south of their village, down the hill past the papermill, then across the bridge and up to Lolly's timeworn millhouse. The man opens the door to their knock, greeting them with bemusement, and, after listening to a brief sales pitch, purchases seeds which he will never use.

Jonathan also takes over Willie's Grit route one week when his brother is ill. The only occurrence of note is a ripped front page and the offering of that paper for half price. The customer, a banker, simply laughs and says, "No; that's all right."

Treasure Island

Mother's and Father's bedroom is off limits to the children. The curtains guarding it against trespass also draw attention to the mysteries which lie within. At least that is the effect they have on Jonathan Hawkins.

He lies in bed thinking of buried treasure, of guarding it with his life and that of beloved Joyce, or storming the camp of would-be friend Long John Silver to forcibly take it, or, perhaps, gently persuading Israel Hands that they should work together with mutual respect and admiration to eventually share it.

There had, indeed, been a buried treasure, once, in the dirt cellar, near the central house-support, its location marked on a sloppily constructed map. Instead of a trunk full of gold doubloons, there was a cigar box containing his most-valued possessions: A round stone, speckled with pinpoint-sized bits of crystal; a secret decoder ring; a plastic whistle; several Cracker Jack prizes; and a few bubble gum cards. This treasure was dug up one day after its burial.

He recalls a treasure he had discovered a long time ago, when he lived in the other village. He and Mother had walked all the way to Grandma's house for a visit, and, while there, he had come across a secret cache of money, thousands of dollars in bills of various denominations. Jonathan had stuffed as much money as he could into his pockets and on the way home had proudly shown it to Mother.

Her reaction was unexpected, however. Instead of joy, there was dismay. "We'll have to return it," she said wearily.

"Why? I found it. Isn't it mine?"

"No. It belongs to Cousin Annie. It goes with her Monopoly game."

Jonathan moaned in disappointment but turned the treasure over to her.

He thinks of his parents' bedroom, of all the whispered conversations which go on in there at night, and wonders what they are trying to keep from the outside world. Father will not even open the curtains so Jonathan can watch him undress, a modesty which seems silly since his pants always hang low and everyone can see the waistband of his boxer shorts.

Now, Jonathan Hawkins approaches the doorway, a sense of adventure urging him slowly on. He slips through the curtains unseen and unheard, barely breathing in order to keep the noise down. More curtains cover the window, so only a small amount of light enters the room. He stands still for a moment, awed by the danger and by the sense of courage infusing his breast.

The room is strangely uninteresting: A bed near the window, a rod in the corner with clothes hung on it, a cedar chest. What draws his attention is a dresser which is flush to the wall near the bed. His gaze skims the objects on top then stops on a small drawer. He opens this, sees it contains mostly socks and is about to close it when a dark rectangular object catches his eye. Hawkins stealthily reaches in and lifts it out. It is Father's wallet.

He opens it to find a section stuffed with bills; is suddenly frightened but unable to stop himself. "Just one," he thinks, "won't hurt anybody. Daddy won't even miss it." He takes a bill out, folds the wallet shut and returns it to the drawer, then escapes back to the safety

141

of his room.

Now that Willie has moved out, to the opposite side of the stairwell, Jonathan Hawkins does not have to worry about sharing the secret of his treasure. He buries it beneath a loose board in the corner, then lies down on his bed, feeling warm and happy, a true brother to Jim Hawkins.

The following morning, before school, Mother angrily confronts the children, demanding to know which one had managed to sink so low as to steal ten dollars from their father.

The words strike Jonathan dumb with panic, and he feels the eyes of the world fall justly and icily on him, freezing him breathless. "I forgot something," he blurts, then spins away and races up the stairs to his buried treasure. Unthinking, he takes it from the hole and stuffs it into his pocket. Not until he is back downstairs does he realize his mistake.

"What's wrong with you?" Mother snaps, grabbing him by the arm. She reaches into his pocket and withdraws the bill. A belt appears from somewhere and she grips it as tightly as she clenches her teeth. With every furious whack, she lets the others know that he is the most wicked child that has ever been born. He leaves the house in tears, walking far behind the others as they head for school, trying to avoid their incurious eyes.

That night, Father calls Jonathan out to the porch and has the boy sit beside him. Then, his eyes focused on some distant trees, he says, "If you ever do anything like that again, I'll have to get a switch and give you a good whipping." Then, in the same calm tone, he asks, "Do you understand?"

Jonathan nods his head and whispers, "Yes." He looks hopefully up at Father's face but finds only coldness there, the same indifference that had made his words seem so dead, and hates him because he doesn't even care enough to get mad.

Jonathan Exposed

Sis is sitting at the dining room table, doing her homework, when Jonathan comes down the stairs in his underwear. He enters the room and squats before the bureau, peeking over at Sis as he goes down, but she doesn't look up from her work. He opens the side door on the bottom, stays there for a long time pretending to search for something, frequently sending sideways glances at Sis who acts as though he isn't there. Finally, he slams the door shut and walks away.

Sis and Father are in the big room at the top of the stairs, rummaging through boxes for some misplaced item. Jonathan is alone in his room, naked, walking back and forth from dresser to bed to dresser to chimney to dresser, stopping near the doorway. He stands still, facing Sis, eyes begging her attention but she still doesn't look. Father also doesn't seem to notice him. Those two keep reaching into boxes, mumbling things like, "Maybe it's in here," continuing not to notice the naked boy. In frustration, he slips away out of sight and into his clothes.

Woodsmen

Father leads the four boys down into the woods. They carry axes and a two-handled saw, looking for suitable trees to chop down and cut up. They settle on a flat area below the upper bank, nearly halfway down the length of the orchard. A tree is felled, perhaps 8 to 10 inches in diameter, the branches trimmed, then Willie and Jonathan are given the responsibility of sawing it into carrying lengths.

Willie takes one handle of the saw, Jonathan the other, and they scratch a guiding cut into the bark then begin a long, arduous descent through the trunk while the others select and chop down other trees. The saw buckles, holds in the damp wood and can't be pulled through. The boys grunt, strain their leg, back, and arm muscles, complain about the impossible task but refuse to admit defeat. Eventually, and mostly through Willie's persistence, they are through the first length. Hours pass slowly; more trees are downed and cut up then lugged on strong shoulders up to the house. Willie and Jonathan attempt to lift one length but are unable to get it off the ground. Joe, amused by their effort, lifts it easily onto his shoulder and hauls it away.

144

Sometime during the afternoon, while the younger boys are working on a trunk and the others are resting nearby, a crashing sound is heard from above. A large deer leaps over the crest of the hill and comes galloping down the bank, almost within arm's length of the humans.

They are silent for a while, stunned by the sight, then Father and the older boys express their amazement and delight. Jonathan says nothing but reruns the scene again and again through his mind, trying to hold it there, to make a permanent imprint. This nature gift has distracted his attention from the unpleasant aspects of his work, and, together with the camaraderie that has developed among them, the crisp air and carpet of brittle leaves, the subdued colors of the woods and sky have made the job almost fun.

After supper, with darkness coming on fast, Jonathan and Father go out to the shed for a final cutting. This is done on a buzzsaw whose pulley-wheel is connected by a wide belt to the wheel rim of an old Ford. The saw consists of a frame anchored to the ground and holding the blade, a moveable bed designed to carry the wood into the cutting edge. A light bulb has been hooked up to the shed's ceiling, its socket on the end of a long electric cord from the house.

It is Jonathan's job to help balance the logs on the bed until they have been cut short enough for Father to manage easily, then later to stack the cut pieces at the rear of the shed. Mostly, he watches, in the dying twilight and then in the darkness, Father pushing the sawbed forward to the frame, the hum of the huge blade changing to a high-pitched whine as the teeth bite into the log, then the piece of firewood falling to the ground. He watches Father late into the evening, the strong body bent slightly and the dark eyes fondly caressing his work, bathed solemnly in the dull-yellow kiss of light. Father is silent, except for an occasional instruction, and, maybe for the first time, Jonathan feels accepted.

The Hunter

Sometimes Father comes home with the large pockets of his hunting jacket filled with rabbits or squirrels. On occasion, there is a pheasant. His double-barreled shotgun carries a burnt odor that intimidates the senses, the smell of steely smoke which permeates every brain cell with the chill of death.

"Daddy, will you take me hunting with you next time?"

"No! You're too young."

"Joe let me go with him."

It is true that Joe had taken Jonathan hunting but had nearly blown his head off. A rabbit, scared out of its wits, had scampered from some underbrush behind them. Jonathan, trailing Joe by a short distance, heard the patter of little feet moving through leaves the same instant that his brother had, and even as Joe was swinging the gun around, Jonathan was flinging himself face-first toward the ground. The blast sounded directly above his head. The pellets whizzed by but struck only leaves and dirt.

"Quick thinking," Joe said in his casual way.

Neither one had ever mentioned the incident to

anyone, so Jonathan knows that cannot be the reason for Father's refusal. Still, he accepts the decision quietly, realizing he will never change that iron-willed mind. There is no longer pleasure in ripping wings off flies or tearing daddy-longlegs apart. He does try to make a slingshot for shooting birds, a bow-and-arrow for rabbits, but these projects fail miserably.

Then, one day, after some discussion at school, Willie, Jonathan, James, and Donald take to the woods. They arrive at the frog pond, weapons resting on their shoulders, and begin stalking their prey. The boys tiptoe up to the edge of the mucky water while the frogs sit with their noses above the surface, watching with disinterested eyes. Clubs are raised then swung down to splat against the water, showering everyone there and smashing frogbrains. When the water is still, Willie scoops the floating bodies up, then carries the amputated legs home for a fried snack.

Jonathan and friends also go there for the simple thrill of killing. With James's BB gun, they take turns sneaking up on their victims, move the barrel down slowly until the muzzle is within an inch or two of a green head, then shoot between the eyes. The frog goes under with a plopping sound, then returns rapidly to float in the slime.

One day, Jonathan visits the frog pond alone, with an old jackknife that Willie had given him. It is sunny and the shallow water carries the stench of decaying matter. The pellet-dotted blobs of clear jelly seen in warmer weather are gone; hatched, the tadpoles lay hidden now in the muck. But Jonathan has not come to this place to catch tadpoles; he has come for bigger game in the interest of science.

The hunt does not last long. A frog sticks its nose above water and he pounces upon it. He places the creature on a flat rock, stretched out on its back with its white belly exposed to the knife. An incision is made from throat to crotch, the flesh pushed aside. Jonathan pokes at the innards and lifts out a white string of intestine on the point of the blade. Probing deeper, he examines other bits of matter but finds his curiosity unsatis-

147

fied.

At last, he comes to a part that is moving; the tiny pink heart desperately pumping blood in a futile effort to keep the body alive. For a long time, Jonathan remains motionless, kneeling beside the rock, watching numbly as the heart beats faster and faster and ever more hopelessly. Then, as gently as possible, he picks the frog up and carries it back to the pond's edge. He squats, lets the frog slip back into what he hopes will be resurrecting water; fights back the fear of what it might really be; watches the frog sink into the blackness and disappear.

"Dear God," he whispers, "I'm sorry. Please don't let him die."

When the frog does not rise back to the surface, either alive or dead, Jonathan leaves. He hurls the knife as far as he can, repeats, "I'm sorry!", then runs down the hill to the stream and up toward the pasture, crying tears of remorse and self-hatred.

Thinking back on this as he sits watching Father puff contentedly on his pipe while Mother sweats over the skinned, disemboweled, stinking corpses in the kitchen, he wonders if he really is unhappy at being told, "You'd just get in the way."

Suzy

Mrs. Wilson writes out an arithmetic problem for the fifth grade then turns to face the class. She says, "Suzy, I want you to come up here and show us how to get the answer."

Suzy's body jerks stiffly to attention in her seat. Her brown eyes plead with Mrs. Wilson, but she rises obediently then walks up the aisle and across the open space to the blackboard. She picks up a piece of chalk then drops her hand back to her side, her shoulders sagging and an expression of hopelessness on her face. For a time, the girl stands staring at the problem.

By now, everyone in the room is watching, anticipating her failure. Mrs. Wilson turns her attention to the fourth grade: "Jonathan, will you please come up here and show Suzy how to solve this problem?" She writes it out on the blackboard, on the next square from Suzy's.

Jonathan walks to the front of the room, picks up a piece of chalk, and slowly but methodically works toward a solution. From the corner of his eye, he notices Suzy working frantically. He maintains a steady pace, simply wanting to obey the teacher, with no intention of showing up the girl.

Suzy finishes the problem first, spins around and rushes back to her seat. A short time later, Jonathan's answer is written beneath the problem. He walks to his seat, noticing a look of horror on Suzy's face.

Mrs. Wilson taps her desk to get everyone's attention, then nods toward the blackboard. "As you see, Suzy finished first." She pauses for effect, then goes on, "But her answer is wrong. Now, Jonathan took longer, but his answer is correct."

The teacher begins a lecture for all three classes, but Jonathan is not paying attention. He is grinning across the rows at Suzy, not gloating but simply enjoying her eccentric misery.

Suzy glares back at him, her eyes fierce and full of loathing.

On Halloween night, the school holds a party in the firehouse. The children play games, bob for apples, eat, and sit around. Near the end, slips of paper are drawn out of a hat. On each slip is written a stunt that a child must perform. Jonathan reaches into the hat, pulls out a slip and hands it to Mrs. Wilson who reads it aloud: "Propose marriage to someone in the room."

Everybody laughs as Jonathan looks around for a suitable mate. He spies Suzy sitting next to Allison, against the far wall. He walks toward her, struggling to keep a straight face.

The two girls are involved in a serious conversation, but Suzy senses that something is amiss and looks up. When she sees him, that expression of naked horror again freezes on her face.

Jonathan drops to his knees, rests his folded hands on her legs, and says, "Will you please marry me?"

Suzy's eyes fill with legions of agony and she yells for all to hear, "No!"

The next day, Jonathan rides his bike past Allison's house just as Suzy is about to knock on the door. They see each other at the same time. Jonathan smiles and waves, but Suzy comes to the edge of the porch to shout after him, "Don't ever ask me to marry you, again!"

Jonathan is in the Christmas play. Rehearsals did not go well because of Suzy's objection to a certain scene, but Mrs. Wilson persuaded her to be a trouper. Suzy is the star, the grandmother of the children in the skit. All she has to do is sit in the middle of the stage, in a rocking chair and wrapped in a shawl, and, after a certain line is spoken, tell them it is bedtime.

The play goes well in the sense that nobody forgets their lines, but Jonathan, sitting on a chair beside his fellow grandchildren, notices a lethargy on the part of the other characters. They are merely going through the motions, reciting lines simply to be done with them while he finds himself completely relaxed and enjoying his part. He wants the parents in the audience to see that he is a good actor, immersed in his role, and that by playing his part so well, they will know how inwardly happy and content he is.

"All right, children, it's time for bed," Suzy says.

Jonathan rises from his chair and marches across the stage to her side. He watches her face go pale, her eyes widen tensely, and her lips tremble, her hands wringing each other beneath the shawl. As he bends down, her eyes shut tightly, her jaw firms as she gnashes her teeth. He plants a kiss on her forehead, then turns and walks offstage. Silence follows him, as though all life on the stage had been sucked away into a vacuum by his departure.

Christmas

Jonathan awakens early in the morning. He dresses without turning on the light, then tiptoes down the stairs to the dining room where the tree is set up near the side door. Presents are spread out beneath it, and there is a beautiful red sleigh in the midst of them, but he does not touch anything. He retreats up the stairs and enters Willie's room; shakes the sleeping boy.

"Willie, get up."

Willie moans. "What do you want?"

"Let's go downstairs and open our presents."

"It's too early. Go back to bed."

"No it isn't. Come on."

"It's still dark." Willie is cross but too tired for a prolonged discussion. "Come back later."

"Will you get up soon?"

"Uhnnnhhh."

Jonathan does not know what this means but hopes for the best. "I'll wait on the stairs." He leaves Willie, to sit on the top step. The hallway is dark, the world outside being stuck somewhere between midnight blackness and the wash of predawn light. He leans forward, elbows on knees, and rests his chin in his hands. After a few minutes of patient waiting, he whispers, "Are you coming, yet?"

There is no reply.

The first Christmas he remembers was easier than this. There had been no foreknowledge or anticipation, only the waking to Willie's joyful noisemaking and the distant glitter of tinsel. He could see the tree from his bed, standing against the far wall of the living room and catching the morning sun on long silver strings and colored globes, Willie hopping from present to present, yelling for him to get up and come see.

Jonathan sloshed out of bed in soaked pajamas, rubbing his sleepy eyes and opening them in wonder. He picked up a tin Tommy gun, trying to grasp the fact that it was his, and shot a round of sparks at Willie. That morning remains like a jeweled spider in the cobwebs of his untidy mind, or like a burst of varicolored fireworks, while the rest fades away.

He makes a second trip down the stairs. Everything remains as it had been around the tree. This time, he passes into the living room, then stands and gazes out the window. The sky has paled slightly and he can make out the shapes of farm buildings to the north. The road runs straight along the pasture fence, almost luminescent, and from the farmhouse lawn comes the ghostly bark of a dog. A shadow moves along the road, becoming more defined the closer it gets. It is Joe. Jonathan climbs the stairs to his room, waits till Joe is in the house and settled in bed, then returns to Willie's side.

"Are you awake, yet?" he shakes Willie, repeating the question until he receives an answer.

"I told you to go back to bed."

"But it's late."

"No it's not. It's still dark."

"The sun's coming up. I can almost see it."

"I said no. We'll wake everybody up and they'll be mad."

Willie rolls over, turning his back to Jonathan. He pulls the blankets over his head and pretends to sleep.

153

Mrs. Walthers, his Sunday school teacher, had given him a book of *365 Bedtime Bible Stories* as a present after the annual Christmas program. A tree had been placed behind the altar near the organ. The presents were under it and were distributed before everyone left for home. There had also been a box of hard candy for each child, with wheels and drops and ribbons, a mixture of sweet smells, and an orange.

But the program had been the main thing; the recitations, the singing, the adoration of Joseph, Mary, and Jesus and their spiritual presence; the bright flame of goodness ignited in everyone.

When they arrived home, Jonathan had proudly showed his book to Mother and Father, expecting praise for his part in the performance. Instead, Father icily said, "What was wrong with you? You kept turning around in your seat and looking at your mother and me. You embarrassed us."

The darkness hangs in the air like smoke. It refuses to rise to let the sun's rays in. Silence deadens the world and the only sounds are echoes in Jonathan's mind. He pounds his knee with his fist, wondering what has happened to Willie, if he has suddenly lost all enthusiasm for life.

Sis is drifting peacefully somewhere, content and unconscious on her sea of Christian love, far beyond the touch of human pleasures. Joe and Teddy are rolling and bumping through a starless sky, aware only of each other. Mother is dreaming of sacrifices and being needed while Father snores busily through giant logs; Jonathan can hear him now, like the sound of an efficient motor.

Meanwhile, in the gloom of Christmas morning, a depressive weight crushes down upon Jonathan, a growing awareness that he is not all that he should be, all that he is expected to be, that he is unfavorably different from the others and is unable to cope with being human, unable to learn the tricks of maturity that everyone else in the family seems to have grasped long ago.

Meanwhile, Willie sleeps on, and on, and on...

Grandma

Jonathan had climbed to the top of the snowbank beside the path. He is about to leap off when he hears Grandma calling from her kitchen door. She beckons to him.

"Jonathan," she says as he nimbly takes the steps to the porch, "would you get me a little water from the cistern? Bobby isn't here."

"Okay," he replies, happy for a chance to impress her with his goodness, pleased that she trusts him with such a difficult task.

She hands him the bucket, cautioning, "Just half a pail."

He takes the bucket out behind the kitchen and sets it beneath the cistern's spout. He jerks the handle a few times to break the ice loose, then pumps out half a pailful. This is carried into the sooty kitchen and lifted atop its stand.

"Dankeschon!" Grandma takes him by the arm then leads him into the dining room and sits him at the table before a bowl of steaming soup. "Eat!" She sits across from him, picks up her magnifying glass and bends over the open Bible.

Jonathan makes a face at the soup. In it are string-beans, corn, pieces of tomato, chunks of animal fat with bits of meat attached, some things he does not recognize. He shivers but spoons some into his mouth. It has the unpleasant texture of Grandma's wrinkled skin and goes down with great difficulty.

"Was ist los?" Grandma stares at him as though he is sick.

"Nothing," he replies politely. "I'm not very hungry."

"Eat! Ist gute for you."

Jonathan sits back in the chair, sighs, pats his stomach, but returns slowly to the chore when he finds no surrender in her good-natured but uncompromising features.

Tennessee Jed

"Layeeeeeeeeeeee... "

"There she goes, Tennessee! Get him!"

A rifle shot with ricochet.

"Got him! Dead center! That's Jed Sloane! Tennessee Jed! Deadliest man with a rifle ever to ride the western plains. Brought to you every day, Monday through Friday, by the bakers of enriched Tip-Top Bread."

Jonathan sits close to the radio, anxiously awaiting his hero's appearance. Tennessee Jed is not just another cowboy; he is the epitome of honesty, courage, and integrity, the supreme marksman.

There are other heros that hold him spellbound after school: Terry and the Pirates, Jack Armstrong, Captain Midnight, Dick Tracy, Superman... These belong to him, alone, because he does not have to share the radio with anyone at suppertime.

Earlier, he shares Mary Noble, Backstage Wife; Stella Dallas; Young Widder Brown; One Man's Family; Lorenzo Jones and his wife Belle; and his favorite soap opera, Just Plain Bill, with Mother as she labors in the kitchen and elsewhere.

Evenings, depending upon whose fingers control the

dial, there are: The Whistler (Jonathan); Truth or Conse-
quences (all); Lum and Abner (Father/Joe); The Thin Man
(Mother/Jonathan); The Quiz Kids (all); Manhattan Merry-
Go-Round (Sis/Jonathan); Mr. Keen, Tracer of Lost Per-
sons (Mother/Jonathan); Mr. and Mrs. North (Mother/Jon-
athan); The Lone Ranger (Father/boys); Judy Canova
(Jonathan); Jack Benny (all); Gangbusters (boys); Fred
Allen (all); Fibber McGee and Molly (all); Amos 'n' Andy
(Father/boys); The Great Gildersleeve (all); Baby Snooks
(Father/Jonathan); Boston Blackie (Jonathan); Bulldog
Drummond (Jonathan); David Harding, Counterspy (Jon-
athan); Duffy's Tavern (Father/boys); Edgar Bergen and
Charlie McCarthy (all); The Fat Man (Jonathan); Lux
Radio Theater (Sis/Jonathan); Inner Sanctum (Jonathan).

Jonathan smiles, recalling the squeaking door, how
it and howling dogs had sent him running through the
darkness to Mother who had left him alone in the house
while she visited Grandma. When she asked what was
wrong, he said, "Nothing."

On Saturday mornings, he listens to The Buster
Brown Show, with Smilin' Ed McConnell, but only if Sis
isn't listening to popular music. Late in the afternoon,
there is The Shadow; evening brings The Grand Ole Opry
whenever Joe isn't home; otherwise, it is dixieland jazz.

But everyone knows who his hero is. Some of the
boys at school, especially younger ones who admire Jonathan, call him Tennessee. The man does not always get
the respect due him, however. After school one rainy
day, Donald began insulting Tennessee, laughing and
coughing as his coarse voice spouted outrages. Soon, he
and Jonathan were rolling on the muddy ground and into
a large puddle, grunting and whining but, as always, causing no physical damage. Donald finally surrendered out
of weariness, not possessing the other's fanatical will to
win. They parted company, but as Donald was about to
enter his house, he shouted a string of curses.

Jonathan's anger had not subsided. His face redden-
ed. "You're not supposed to swear," he yelled. "Don't
you ever read the Bible?" He was pleased with his retort, knowing that Tennessee Jed would be proud of him.

Today, Tennessee must prevent the Dalton gang

158

from renewing the war between the states, an event which would enable Nick Dalton to take over the federal government. At the moment, Cookstove, Sheriff Tate, and Jose are about to be hanged by the outlaws.

Nick Dalton boastfully says, "You've seen men hang before, Cookstove. A good slap starts your horses running, leaving you three swinging in the breeze."

Cookstove bravely replies, "I ain't scared of dyin', Dalton, but I'm sure entitled to a last word."

They talk awhile. Dalton admits he is hanging them to make it look like the work of their enemies, thus precipitating a battle which will draw federal troops from Louisiana, leaving none there to put down the riots he will start when he moves into that state.

Finally, Dalton says, "Okay, men, when I give the word, yank on those ropes, chase the horses from under Cookstove, Sheriff Tate, and Jose." Pause. "Now!"

The sound of a slap is followed by the sound of galloping horses, then, "Layeeeeeeeee... "

"It's Tennessee's yodel," Dalton says, cringing.

A rifle shot, with continuing yodel.

Another outlaw exclaims, "He's cut Cookstove's rope. With his rifle."

A second shot, with continuing yodel.

"Jose! He cut Jose down, too!"

A third shot, sounding like a dud, with continuing yodel.

Dalton says, "he cut them all down. Take no chances with Tennessee's rifle, men. Clear out!"

Panic ensues and the outlaws ride off.

Tennessee rides up, says, "Whoa, Smokey," and dismounts, as does Snake. They loosen the ropes, allowing the Dalton gang to escape. The three hanged men gradually revive.

"One time we was almost too late, Snake," Tennessee says.

"Don't say that, son. When I saw them three yanked into midair, I thought they was goners."

"Some might call it luck," Tennessee says. "I say the Lord was doin' the sightin' that time."

Jonathan smiles because Tennessee has said just

the right thing.

When Cookstove asks why he showed up when he did, Tennessee replies, "The Lord willed it, Cookstove."

The smile grows and Jonathan fills with warmth. He is happy that he and Tennessee Jed have the Lord for a mutual friend.

Where the Soul Never Dies

Every Sunday morning, Jonathan and Sis walk a mile and a half to church, where they attend services then stay for Sunday school. They sing hymns with the congregation, pray to God, listen to the sermon and drop money into the collection plate. In Sunday school, James and Sammy are also in his class, though Jonathan is the only one who behaves like a Christian child and does not drive the teacher to distraction. He loves the beautiful color pictures in their lessons, especially those of Jesus.

On the way to and from church, brother and sister discuss religion.

"Are you saved?" Sis asks.

"I don't know."

"If you were saved, you'd know it in your heart. You have to be born again. Spiritually. If you're not born again, you won't be saved and you'll go down below and burn in fire forever."

Jonathan decides that he wants to be born again but keeps the decision to himself. As he walks, he thinks about the requirements, and the possibilities that go with success: Self-sacrifice, meekness; dedication; a happy eternity with God.

161

At home, he often reads from his 365 Bedtime Bible Stories. He is in awe of Solomon's wisdom, Samson's strength, David's and Daniel's courage, but mostly the goodness of Jesus. He promises God that he will always be like Jesus: Good, kind, gentle, forgiving. And now that he no longer has Willie to talk to in bed at night, he often turns to God for companionship.

In the spring, he discovers a gently sloping hillside in the woods near the creek, covered thickly with yellow adder's-tongue. There is also a sparse growth of trees whose branches and leaves form a green canopy over his head. Birds and squirrels move briskly through the treetops, making pleasant sounds, and still higher are invisible angels, protectors of this hallowed ground. Jonathan decides that this will be his chapel in the woods, the place where he can talk privately to God and be saved from the fires of Hell.

Circa Epilogue

The pain always comes first, a longing for something that is beautiful and eternal. I see my salvation in the smile of an adoring child, the simple, uncomplicated purity of innocence and trust. I build my dreams on fragmented shadows which I transform into lovely, perhaps false, images. Maybe all of our images are false, our vision impaired by centuries of subjective, simplistic logic that we call common sense but which is really lazy, shallow thinking and the unqualified acceptance of myth as fact. We don't know enough about ourselves, as a species or as thinking beings, to judge customs and beliefs; we do not know enough about God to compare one religion with another. Who are we to say that cannibalism is worse than an atomic bomb, that slavery is worse than starvation, that nakedness is worse than a large bank account, or that a thief is worse than a drunk driver? Who among us is honest enough, or far enough removed from the scene, to see the truth?

I love children, especially the shy, those whose spirits suffer daily from the rigors and associations of life, who would be gentle and kind if the world would let them; those whose purity of spirit is tinged with an underlying mixture of black feelings and a sense of always standing on the edge of an abyss, always on the verge of tumbling down into the dark unknown.

There are children of incredible beauty, but a man is not allowed to see this or remark on it, unless he wishes to have his manhood challenged, or his morality, or his sanity. But only a person who truly loves children can appreciate their sensuous qualities, which is one reason why children have always been closer to women. Women are permitted, even encouraged, to love the entire child and not just his performance. Those who worship machismo loathe these feelings and consider them unnatural for a man; they fear that any display of tenderness or affection for children will be seen as effeminate, a sign of weakness, and they are afraid to ask themselves where their concepts of masculinity come from, how they evolved in our culture, who has the authority to define these concepts and impose them upon us, who has given these people the right to treat with contempt those who have the courage to think for themselves. I see a scale of rejection, where the more one fears the sensuous qualities of children, the more he tends to reject children, believing he is protecting his own masculinity in the process. A certain philosophy results from this. In its basest form, it states: "It is a woman's duty to nurture and a man's duty to make war."

There is a new boy on the block. He is about ten years old. I saw him leaning against a pillar, talking to a friend about baseball cards. His voice was soft and pensive, unconsciously seductive. Blond hair fell over his ears, hiding his face, but a glimpse showed it to be beautiful. More than innocent, it had frozen the honesty, the faith, the gentleness that existed in his mind into an exquisite sculpture. The boy wore short pants, a T-shirt, and sneakers. His skin was honey-colored and scrubbed clean, his eyes were shiny with uninhibited love for his friend, and I wished he would look at me that way.

But I have noticed a gradual change in him, a toughening process as he adapts to a new environment.

164

The innocence is still there, but it has become grim, as though intuiting a darker side to life. His facial lines have tightened; his jaw is now firm and defiant.

Today, his green eyes met mine briefly. They were set in a perpetual squint of unhappiness and they had hardened considerably. I smiled, hoping those eyes would soften, but they didn't. I wanted to reach out and touch him, lay my hand on his shoulder and heal him, but couldn't.

It is peaceful in the twilight. Clouds gather above the mountains across the river, balls of pink and gray fluff against a darkening sky. The air is cool and sounds travel far; children playing games in alleys, giggling at whispered repartee, hiding from grownup eyes, dancing through shadows, exploring new worlds faster than their minds can structure them.

Up one street and down another as night settles in. A group of little girls has gathered in front of a grocery store. One is yelling to a boy who has fled the scene; "Come back! Cindy wants to kiss you!"

They laugh and make a racket. The storekeeper comes out to chase them away. There is a gasp. One girl exclaims to another, "You said a bad word!"

The other girl puffs up her chest then lets the word explode from her lungs; "Shit!"

The old man hobbles after them, but they are too quick.

The miscreant backs away, taunting him with a string of obscenities. "I'm not afraid of you, you fuck, you prick, you... !"

The girls dash around the corner. He stays awhile, peeking around the building, hoping they will return so he can grab his tormentor.

I walk through the small gathering. The girls are around nine and ten years old. A pretty child with sandy hair and sensitive brown eyes gazes up at me. There is no fear that I might grab her and turn her over to the old man. She is merely seeking my reaction, trying to determine what I think of them, just as I am trying to read her mind. There is no guilt, either, just a gentle

165

seeking for an answer I cannot give.

They are silent now, subdued and overwhelmed by themselves. The words have all been used up, have served their purpose. Their power has dissipated. There is nothing more the children can do. But they fail to see the truth: They are not just words, they are a philosophy, a way of life, a tactic for survival, a mode of thinking that has captured them and holds them in a bondage they cannot escape. It is the character of their existence that extends beyond words, but the words are what mark them. They are weapons, expressions of the ugliness, the bitterness, the loathing, the unthinking violence that is their inheritance. And those who insist that the words are only words fail to see what else they are and do not care to trace them back to their origins in the children's minds and lives. They fail to see what slaves these brutal words have made of the children.

I walk to the end of the street, then return, but most of the girls are gone. A boy is calling the last one home, threatening to lock her out if she doesn't hurry. She walks ahead of me, her pace quickening as she sees her brother leaning out the door, silhouetted by a light from inside the house. At the end, she is nearly running. I wonder what it is she is running to.

I want to save her and the others but dare not try.

Paul is not a handsome boy, but he has beautiful puppy-dog eyes which are constantly laughing and begging for love. His mother and father are dead, and, though he lives with his older sister, it is me to whom he has come for that love. We watch ballgames on TV, snack together, talk about favorite TV heros or sports' stars, or I will give him piggyback rides around the apartment. Sometimes he will throw his arms around my neck and quickly but painfully say, "I love you." He will sit on my lap and make me give him bearhugs until he says uncle. He will do none of these things when his friends are with him; then he will insult and ill-treat me, share in their smutty jokes and manly boasting and demand money from me. But he will do these things secure in the knowledge that I understand his motivation and will not later reject him for his bad behavior.

Neither is Paul a sensuous boy; he is too prone to dirt and scrapes, too full of energy and rapid movement to be appreciated as artwork, his spirit too often bright to be seductive. Yet, he has his dark moods, perhaps when life has been unjust to him or when he pauses to think deeply about himself, or when he has a question he is afraid to ask; then he will settle somberly onto my lap and sink into me as our spirits meld.

Later, in the filtered gloom, we awaken to the old sense of each other as just friends but with a new awareness of our growing need for each other, the support and comfort we find in one another, the delicate trust and the fear that goes with it. But I wonder if I am leading him down a wrong path, one from which there is no returning. I ask myself if he sees me as a father-figure or as a lover. I ask myself how I see him.

I love Paul, but can there be love without desire? Is there a craving I am not aware of, or am conscious of but sublimate, perhaps forcing myself to see it as something else? The question progresses, extends into the taboo. Can a father truly love his children without experiencing some form of desire, even if only on a subliminal level? Is this the drive that keeps parents from abandoning or murdering their children, and is it thus a significant factor in the perpetuation of the species? Is it this drive which causes fathers to wrestle with their children, to tickle them and carry them on their shoulders, to hug and kiss them or even take them to ballgames; which causes mothers to dote on their little boys when they and fathers have come to impasses, the drive whose very existence must be denied?

I have my own theory. Children unknowingly recognize the sensual interest their parents unknowingly have in them, and they play up to it, learn to be seductive and tender, and from this learn to respect and accommodate others.

It is this way with Paul. With his friends, he is rough and nasty, distancing himself from warmth and affection because these feelings would destroy the shared psyche their world has misconstrued. And it is also my theory that children wish they could be gentle, tender, and sensitive; that, if given a choice, they would reject all forms of violence in favor of peace and caring.

Because of Paul's love for roughhousing and boyish games, I assumed he was inured to bloodshed. Such is not the case. He had asked me for a banana, one day, then asked me to peel it for him because he always made a mess of it. Joking, I took a knife and made a cut across the nub end, saying, "First, you have to slit its throat."

Paul's eyes opened wide and a look of horror came to his face. I knew I had made a mistake. I could see, in his mind, blood gushing from the wounded banana, running down my hand and dripping into a huge puddle on the floor.

I watched his expression change to one of embarrassment. But I was angry with myself, remembering a scene from my own childhood and how one does not forget:

The Executioner

Cousin Howard's father had invited Jonathan's family to spend a day on his farm. Only Father and Mother knew, as they drove northward, the real purpose of the visit. Mr. Williams, because of health problems, had made plans to move to Arizona and, since he could not take his three dogs with him, had asked Father to put them away.

When they arrived at the farm, they were shown into the house by Mrs. Williams, taken through a large summer-kitchen where the sickening-sweet smell of rotting garbage assaulted Jonathan's nostrils. There was a light lunch, then the children went outside to play. Father and Mr. Williams disappeared behind the barn, Father carrying his double-barreled shotgun.

As soon as the men were out of sight, Cousin Howard's older brother, Albert, directed the boys to follow him. While Sis and Mother joined Mrs. Williams on the front porch, the boys slipped into the barn. They were led to double doors at the rear, where a large gap allowed them to look out at a bare patch of ground and a wooden fence that separated it from a small apple orchard.

169

Cousin Howard stretched out on the floor and the others stacked themselves above him, according to height: Jonathan, Willie, Cousin Albert, Teddy, then Joe.

Jonathan saw an old hound standing wobbly-legged near the fence, one end of a string around its neck and the other fastened to a post, Father bending down to place a scrap of meat in front of it. That done, he stood erect again then took a step backward, swinging the shotgun up as he moved. Mr. Williams stood off to the side.

The dog lowered its head to sniff the meat, its eyes dull with age and infirmity. Then a loud explosion so startled Jonathan that something black, like a curtain, cut through his mind and blinded him. When vision returned, he saw the dog lying on its side. Father and Mr. Williams were standing beside it. The dog's head was pointed toward the barn, eyes closed, mouth formed in a wavy line. The men bent over the body, muttering to each other.

Jonathan remembered a headless chicken running wildly across their lawn, dripping blood upon the grass while Father stood calmly watching, axe in hand, and the chicken's head lay at the base of the chopping block. He wondered how anyone could be so cold-hearted as to kill, but he knew that he was just as guilty as Father.

He slid out from under the stack of boys, turned and ran from the barn. As he raced toward the front of the house, frogs hopped inside his head, frantically seeking the foul pond that would save them.

Sis was sitting on the edge of the porch, her face pale and eyes wide with apprehension. Mother and Mrs. Williams were sitting on chairs nearby, talking softly. Jonathan sat beside Sis but neither one spoke.

He listened for the frogs as they continued their search through his mind, but there was only a depressing silence there, too. He wondered if Father would come to be haunted by these dogs.

He peeked around the side of the building and saw the men leading a second hound from an outbuilding and toward the rear of the barn. This one was younger. It wagged its tail and licked Mr. Williams's hand.

170

"They got another one," Jonathan said.

Sis did not reply.

When the second blast came, he noticed her body jerk, but she made no other response. He hoped that, if she needed comforting, she would go to Mother, because he did not know what to say to her.

The third dog, a young terrier, sensed that it was in for a bad time. Mr. Williams tried to assure it that everything was okay, but it whined and struggled.

A long time passed before a third shot was heard. A high-pitched yelp followed. Someone shouted, then there was a second blast and more yelping. The noise grew louder, coming toward the house.

Father yelled, "Stop him!" He came into view around the corner of the barn. The boys rushed out to join the chase. It went in circles for a while, out in the open, then moved along the side of the house. Someone crashed into a hedge. Joe yelled, "I've got him!", but there was a squeal of pain as the dog broke away.

It came into the front yard and ran in circles there.

"Come on! Get him!" Father yelled as he went by, but neither Jonathan nor Sis made a move to help.

The dog burst through a flower bed, then back into the yard. A splotch of red showed against the black of its front paw, while the severed string dangled from its neck.

They finally trapped it against the hedge. The dog whimpered, its tail stuck between its legs, but Mr. Williams picked it up and carried it away toward the barn, cooing to it gently.

Later, in the car, Father explained that the terrier had moved just as he pulled the trigger. The shot which struck the dog's paw had also severed the string. "I wish it hadn't happened but that's the way it is."

That night, Jonathan sat alone on the porch. The frogs had calmed down and were hopping lazily through a field of high grass. He knew that, if he tried, he could make the dogs appear, their snouts pointing at the moon, and he would be able to hear their mournful howling, but he would be unable to place them inside the frame of Father's mind.

171

Dish Washer

Mother has gone shopping with Uncle Lou, leaving behind a pile of dishes and silverware to be washed later. None of the others are home, otherwise Sis might consider doing them. Jonathan knows it will be late when Mother gets back, that she will be tired but obliged to fix supper after the groceries are put away and the dishes washed. He thinks about this and decides to wash them for her.

He fills the basin with hot water and soap, then begins the unpleasant task. The dishes contain the last remnants of dinner, that part of the food left untouched by an earlier scraping, and he tries hard not to look at it. But, while swishing the dishcloth across the plates in the soapy water, he feels bits of corn and specks of other edible matter brush against his fingers, thick sauce ooze between and around them, stuff left behind yet connected to other stuff which has been in people's mouths. He closes his eyes, grimaces, holds his breath against the odor, but bravely continues the struggle. The more dishes that are washed, the thicker becomes the gross matter in the water, and the more nauseated Jonathan becomes. Solid food is stuck between the tines of forks;

172

butter and mustard remain on knives; but the spoons are the most glaring reminders of things which have been in people's germ-infested mouths and he handles them with the greatest care and delicacy of all.

At last, he is finished with the washing and tosses the water off the porch onto the rear lawn. He fills the basin with cold rinse water, puts in the dishes and silverware, then takes them out for drying.

When the job is finished, he heaves a sigh of relief and allows himself a smile, knowing that Mother will be pleased.

He goes to the living room to read comic books and wait for her. Every now and then, he returns to the kitchen to look out the door window at the long stretch of road to the south. Soon, he stays there for longer and longer periods, thinking that Uncle Lou's black coupe should be coming into view at any moment. But it does not come, and he feels certain that something bad has happened to them: There has been an accident; they have gotten lost and cannot find the way home; Mother has decided that she will never return home again because she is fed up with them, especially with him. The sun falls toward the mountains, touches the bumpy horizon, and still there is no car. His worry grows almost to panic.

Then, suddenly, like a bright beam of sunlight finding a hole in the clouds on a gloomy day, the car appears down beyond the orchard, snailing along and growing slowly bigger and bigger until it reaches full size. It slows even more and makes a troubled turn into the driveway.

"Mommy," he says as she climbs out of the car, "I washed the dishes for you." He is unable to contain his enthusiasm and smiles upward as he awaits her response.

She simply grunts and walks to the rear of the car. Uncle Lou joins her there, his round face grim and his equally round body swaying. He opens the trunk and Mother retrieves two bags of groceries; Jonathan takes another.

They walk in line to the porch; Mother first, then Uncle Lou, then Jonathan. Mother climbs the two steps.

173

Uncle Lou follows but falters. His body totters precariously on the bottom step.

"Watch yourself," Mother says.

Jonathan realizes that the warning is meant for him, but it is unnecessary. He has been watching Uncle Lou's back closely, and when it suddenly retreats downward in his direction, he deftly sidesteps the falling body.

Uncle Lou has curled himself into a ball, and when he strikes the hard ground of the driveway, there is barely a sound. He rolls halfway over onto his bald head, then rocks back and stretches out flat.

Mother puts the bags down, descends the stairs and helps Uncle Lou to his feet, then struggles up the steps into the house with him.

The man does not look well, and Jonathan asks, "What's wrong with him?"

"He's been drinking," Mother says matter-of-factly.

Jonathan does not know what to make of the situation. He has seen inebriated men outside the two taverns in town and at ballgames, but, until now, he has never seen one of his relatives that way and isn't sure if he is supposed to be disgusted or amused. The closest he had previously come to a drunk experience in the family was a night Father came home from a union meeting in a good mood and handed him a roll of black friction tape, saying, "This is for you."

When he told his brother of the curious incident, Willie merely shrugged and said, "He's drunk."

Willie had not been the least bit upset, so Jonathan decides there is no reason for him to be upset by Uncle Lou's condition. He is relieved, though, that no one outside the family had seen him like that.

While Mother sits Uncle Lou at the table and fixes him some coffee, Jonathan carries in the groceries. He decides it would not be wise to bring to her attention, again, his afternoon's labor of love. He hopes, when the situation improves, that she will notice on her own, but she doesn't, and he is disappointed.

The Joke

"There was this farmer," Joe says. "He had a cabbage garden. One night a rabbit came and ate one of
them."

Sis leans toward him in the front seat while Willie
leans forward from behind.

"In the morning, he went out and saw that one of
the cabbages was missing. He tried to figure out what
had happened to it but couldn't."

Sis glances back at Jonathan and smiles sympathet-
ically.

He groans, clutching his stomach. His head reels
from the fumes and the swaying of the rickety old car.
The headlights flash across trees and houses and empty
space and dully against the macadam to be thrown back
at him at disconcerting angles. "I don't feel good."

"We'll be home soon. You'll feel better then."

"Next night, the rabbit came back. This time he
ate two cabbages. When the farmer went out to hoe his
garden in the morning, he saw they were gone, but he
couldn't figure out what had happened to them."

"We'll never get home."

"Shhhhh. Listen to Joe."

175

"The next night, the rabbit came back and ate three cabbages... "

" ...night, the rabbit came back and ate twenty-three cabbages. In the morning, the farmer came out to look at his garden and saw they were gone, but he could not figure out what had happened to them."

"Just tell us the end," Willie says. "I don't want to hear all of it."

"Be patient. I'm getting there."

Ghostly structures line the highway, homes of the nameless dead. Jonathan thinks that he and they might have something in common. Were they killed by the same poisonous fumes that are infusing his system? Did their heads go spinning off their shoulders as his is about to do? Did their bile back up on them to rise in their throats until death had the sourest taste imaginable? As though in answer to his fears, a graveyard suddenly looms to their right, cold stones climbing the gentle slope of a hill and silhouetted against the moon. Joe breaks away briefly for another joke. "Bet you can't guess how many people live there."

Sis turns her head to gaze through the window. "I give up. How many?"

Jonathan slides up on the seat and peeks out to make a hurried count of headstones. Willie has the same idea. He climbs over his brother for a better view.

"None," Joe says. "They're all dead." He laughs, Sis giggles, and Willie retreats to his side of the car, pounding the seat in mock anger.

"Ohhhhhhh. My stomach."

"Anyway, the next night the rabbit came back and ate twenty-five... "

The joke isn't finished yet, but Sis already thinks it's hilarious.

Willie has fallen asleep.

Joe never tells jokes to Jonathan. Only to Sis, Mother, or Teddy. Jonathan thinks it would be nice if he looked back once and said to him and him alone, "The next night the rabbit came back and ate seventy-six cabbages." Instead, he says it to Sis.

Joe's presence fills the car; his laughter and his power. Still, he fails to notice Jonathan. "Why can't you look back for just one second?" the child pretends to ask. "To see if I'm still alive." But Joe is aware of only Sis as the joke goes on and on. " ...and the farmer could not... "

The road twists and turns through woodland, goes down in a sudden dip but the bile stays up and he has to swallow it. They rise toward a pale moon floating behind a web of tree branches.

"The next night the cabbage came and ate ninety-two rabbits." Joe peeks over at Sis, and Jonathan sees tears in his eyes. Joe returns his attention to the road, his huge body shaking with laughter. "In the morning... " He has a coughing spell and can't go on.

Sis, too, is laughing, her body doubled over and her head nearly touching the dashboard. She peeks back at Jonathan who sees that tears also fill her eyes.

" ...the farmer went out... " The last word is an explosion, then coughing stops him again.

Willie is snoring, unaware of it all.

Joe has himself under control again. He says, rather quickly, " ...and saw they were gone, and he couldn't figure out what had happened to them."

Once again, he joins Sis in hearty laughter.

Jonathan wonders if the joke will ever end, or if it will go on forever, like this ride. "Sis, my stomach," he complains, but they continue to ignore him.

"The next night the rabbit came and... "

At last, the long, straight stretch of road south of home. He takes a deep breath and some of the discomfort goes away. The road becomes a silvery carpet leading to solace. He sees the light of Grandma's dining room window and knows she is in there reading her Bible. Lamplight shines through the living room window of his own house, splashing weakly out onto the lawn. Mother will be in there, knitting, or reading a book.

Joe slows the car and prepares to turn into the

driveway, saying, "Now, the next night the rabbit came and ate one hundred and seven cabbages," just as Willie sits up suddenly with pretended awareness, as though he had been following the joke all along. The car creeps along the driveway, along the front of the house, and everyone is now fully awake, breathless for the climax. "The farmer went out and saw that all those cabbages were missing."

He stops the car and Jonathan nearly bumps his nose against the side of Sis's head. Willie's chin is resting on top of the backrest.

Joe turns toward Sis but has to look away to keep from laughing. He bangs his fist against the dashboard then rests his chest upon the steering wheel, and, his body heaving spasmodically, giggles and squeals, "And to this day, that farmer doesn't know what happened to his cabbages."

Swimmers

On a warm June afternoon, Jonathan went with Willie, James, Andy, Fred, and Donald to the creek to swim at the second bed of rock. The boys stripped off their clothes and dove in, to be carried downstream by the current then to swim back up through the choppy water and patches of foam. They became underwater torpedoes, aiming themselves at the living targets there, or diving to intercept the submarine bodies.

Jonathan felt guilty at first, as though he was committing a crime for which he could be arrested. He worried about an airplane which passed high overhead, and cars which climbed to the hilltop above the mill to be glimpsed briefly between trees. An electric tension passed through him, needing release which came with a joyful shout of, "Jesus Christ!"

The other boys turned to look at him in shocked amazement. James said, "I thought you didn't swear."

Jonathan grinned sheepishly and replied, "Oh, is that swearing?"

No one found enough interest to commence a discussion of the subject, much to his relief. He gradually relaxed and lost his feeling of guilt; the swimming

became a pleasant matter of moving through cool, sooth-
ing water.

Some boys, who lived on top of the hill across the
creek and beside the state highway, came to share the
fun. Two of these were older boys, and Jonathan noticed
that each had thick, curly hair growing on his lower ab-
domen. He grimaced, hoping that such an unsightly
growth would never disfigure his body that way.

One boy had a penis which reached almost to his
knees, bringing much attention and comment from the
others and causing Donald to ask how he managed to
keep all of it tucked inside his bathing suit. Donald, encouraged by everyone's interest, went on to remark,
"Charlie fucked a girl, last night."

While the others quietly discussed this accomplishment of an older teenager, Jonathan sought the significance of the act within himself. He stretched out on
the flat rocks to let the sun dry his goosepimpled flesh.
For a moment, the meaning was bright and clear in his
mind, but it quickly dissolved, leaving a residue which he
tried to build upon. He envisioned Charlie inserting his
penis into the crack between some girl's buttocks and
somehow enjoying it.

Charlie, he realized, must be brave if he had
actually accomplished this feat and must be someone to
look up to with admiration. Because of this, when Jonathan decided to test himself a week later by attempt-
ing to swim for the first time the couple of hundred
feet from the bed of rock beside the sand bar to the
waterfall below the dam, it was Charlie whom he asked
to escort him.

"All right," Charlie said, "but if you get tired,
don't panic and start grabbing for me, because I'll have
to knock you out."

"Okay," Jonathan happily agreed.

He did a shallow dive from the rocks, then floated
a ways before starting an overhand stroke. Charlie
caught up and stayed at his side, watching grimly, but
Jonathan completed stroke after stroke with a strength
and determination he never realized he possessed. When
they reached the falls, they climbed up to a fairly flat

180

surface where some other boys were resting.

"Not bad," Charlie said.

"It wasn't hard," he replied, noting a touch of disappointment on the older boy's face. "I'm not even tired."

Charlie shrugged his shoulders, though it was barely noticeable, and gazed back at the small crowd on the sand bar. It occurred to Jonathan that Charlie had probably been hoping for a failure so he could have played the part of the hero.

Carnival

Jonathan arrives early, while the men are setting up the booths, tables, and lights. He is appointed official errand boy and odd-job worker. Payment is an evening's supply of free ice cream (within limits, he later learns).

Since he only has four quarters to spend, he holds onto them as long as he can. Bingo tempts him with its shelves of varied prizes and string of glittering lights around the square of tables; the women and girls cheerfully scrutinizing their cards. One game brings quick failure, and he sets his sights elsewhere.

He proves to James that he can get free ice cream, but, since it is his third trip there and the evening is still young, he is advised to exercise restraint from that point on.

He leaves the ice cream booth to walk the length of stalls lined beside the schoolhouse, each with its own spinning wheel and array of prizes. He pauses in front of the wine booth, thinking he might try to win a bottle for Father, but is sent away. A ring-toss game takes more of his money, then, late in the evening, after aimless wandering with friends, he finds himself with Willie at the ball-toss booth.

There are four stuffed-cat dolls on the table, the prizes stacked on shelves and hung on the canvas walls behind them. Jonathan pays for three balls then steps back to make his first throw.

Barney, the man in charge of that booth and one of the unwashed alcoholics whom Sis emphatically detests, offers gentle encouragement; "Come on, Jonathan, you can do it."

He smiles as he winds up. He likes Barney and can't understand why Sis doesn't. This gives him a sense of independence, the idea that he is his own man, and also a determination to please this new friend. There is an obstacle, however; a board atop the front of the booth where transactions are made. He can see over it well enough but realizes it will inhibit his delivery. Still, he fires the first ball with all his might. It smashes squarely into the midsection of a cat and sends it flying off the table.

"Hey! Good!" Barney exclaims, his unshaved face grinning. "Do it again."

The second ball takes the next cat but, despite encouragement from Barney and other spectators, he sees an insurmountable problem: Two cats and only one ball. He aims carefully for the middle, thus losing a little steam from his throw, and, though the ball strikes exactly where he wants it to, he manages merely to spin them around.

His prize is a whip. He runs to show it to Andy and James, but the latter is nowhere to be found. Instead, he comes upon a fight in the middle of the carnival grounds near the bingo tables. Everyone there has stopped what they were doing to watch. The combatants are Buck and James's father, and each is too drunk to hurt the other. After a few minutes of ineffectual wrestling, they wind up beneath a bingo table. Buck crawls out from under, gets to his feet and staggers up the road away from the carnival. James's father remains where he is, having fallen asleep, and the play continues.

Jonathan wonders if James had left in embarrassment. He wonders, too, if the boy's father is as mean as his own, since he has noticed in James nervous habits similar to his own, namely a wheezing squeak James always manages to turn into a hum, thus disguising the habit.

He and Andy break the whip, so they head back to the ball-toss booth. This time he wins a paper lei.

After a final visit to the ice cream booth, he and Willie walk home through the darkness.

Baseball

When the village team plays away games, Uncle Lou packs Cousin Bob, Willie, and Jonathan into the coupe and takes them there. For home games, the boys simply walk upstreet to the ballfield.

The diamond is set back a few hundred feet from the road. A cornfield cuts straight across from right field through center then continues out deeper and deeper into left. There is a wire backstop behind homeplate, and more wire fencing extends down the third and first base lines. Snow fencing runs out to short right field, past the scoreboard, where it joins the foul line near the cornfield. Behind this fence is the town dump. There is no fence along the left field line, only a foul pole at its deepest point.

Since Jonathan is usually the first boy there, he almost always wins the job of ball chaser. His duties are to chase and find foul balls hit over the fencing, balls which usually wind up in the high weeds or the dump, and to make sure that others do not try to steal them.

Behind the plate, for the home team, is Jake Woodward, the finest catcher in the league despite the fact that he has only one lung.

On first base is Lefty Albert, whose speed and power are legendary. Jonathan has seen him beat out routine grounders to the infielders. Lefty has several fingers missing, the result of an accident with dynamite, but this does not inhibit his play. He owns the farm where Ernest had lived. Jonathan and Willie visit him there, to jump from a beam into the hayloft or to watch him milk cows. The boys are taught, by hands-on experience, about electric fences. Lefty is cheerful and has nicknamed Jonathan, "Plastic Man", after the boy's favorite comic book character.

On second base is Jonathan's favorite player. Jim Ward is a quiet, decent man, very much like Tennessee Jed, and just as handsome. He is very fast and makes spectacular catches of line drives headed for right field. His only defensive problem is a weak arm, but his intelligent play compensates for this. At bat, he is a line drive hitter. Joe claims that Jim could do even better but his wrists are too quick for this league and he sometimes cannot adjust to inferior pitching.

At shortstop is Gary "Slingshot" Bucholsky, whose nickname comes from his throwing style. Gary is a cousin to Frankie, Jonathan's classmate. He is one of the few ordinary players on the team.

On third is Ed Simmons, a fine defensive player who consistently hits for a high average. Ed has the best arm of any player in the league and, like Jim Ward, is as handsome as a movie star.

The left fielder is Karl Goetz, a long-armed, long-legged, ordinary player.

In center is Jack Krisniski, a war hero. Jack is a big man with the power to hit home runs, and the other teams' outfielders always play him back almost to the cornfield. Although Jack had been wounded in the war and has trouble throwing, he is frequently used as a relief pitcher.

The right fielder is Dick Van Allen, the team clown. Dick is such a good fielder, making somersaulting catches which Jonathan tries to emulate at home when bouncing his rubber ball off the house, that he sometimes sits in a rocking chair in the field late in games

186

when his team is far ahead. Strong winds and bright sunlight do not hamper his fielding, but Dick is unable to play unless he is drunk. The fans understand this and love him all the more for it.

The main pitcher is Joe Ressler, a tall, lean left-hander who had once turned down an offer to pitch for the New York Yankees. He is also a quiet man and the best pitcher anywhere outside the major leagues. Joe works at the papermill and had once visited Father on union business when Jonathan was sick. Jonathan was lying on the living room couch, his head near the smelly garbage pail in case he had to vomit, while the men talked in the dining room. Joe had noticed him and said to Father, "The little fella isn't feeling well, huh?"

Father explained about the illness then offered Joe a seat at the table.

Jonathan had felt both pleased and embarrassed by the man's attention but wished he had come in and talked baseball with him.

The manager is Arthur Green, a dignified, elderly man who mostly lets the players play their game, making few tactical changes. It is he who doles out the money after the games to the players from the collection box, who pays the ball chasers each a quarter and decides whether or not they deserve any old balls or broken bats.

The whole of the team is greater than its parts. They lift each other, function as a unit, and are the best team the league has ever known.

Their chief rival comes from two villages away, a milltown where people are rough and uncouth. The players are a shady-looking bunch who would never win a game if it wasn't for certain unscrupulous umpires who always manage to work these two teams' games. This team's fans are also worthy of contempt and can always be seen jeering and hooting from behind home plate all the way down the left field line, except when the collection box comes around and they conveniently disappear.

Despite the disconcerting behavior of rival fans, incompetent umpires, and ignoble competitors, the home team wins the league championship.

The Negro

Some disparaging remarks had been made about negroes. When Mr. Walthers, the Sunday school superintendent, learned of this, he gathered all the students together and lectured them on the subject.

"You shouldn't look down on negroes," he said, pacing back and forth at the front of the church. "They are just as good as you and me. There are negroes who are teachers, and doctors, and scientists. There is nothing wrong with negroes, and you shouldn't call them names. Not only that," he concluded, leaning over the front pew and smiling benignly, "we should admire their natural sense of rhythm. Some of them are magnificent tap dancers."

This pleasant thought is on Jonathan's mind as he watches the negro center fielder glide gracefully in and to his right to backhand a line drive off Joe's bat. He believes the speed and beauty of movement are expressions of the colored youth's natural sense of rhythm: At bat, the tall, lean body is taut, upright, yet poised to spring like a panther at the incoming pitch, an expression of grim determination on the dark face; the muscles of the arms ripple as he swings and connects to send a

long drive into left-center; the long legs carry him ga-
zelle-like around first, past second, and safely into third.

After the game, the negro comes over to the home
team's bench to shake hands with the defeated players.
Teddy takes the brown hand and congratulates the vic-
tor, and it makes Jonathan happy that his brother appreciates at least this one negro.

He steps up close to the two teenagers, observing
without inhibition the brown hand which clasps the white
one, and he wonders with a shiver how it would feel to
touch the strange skin. He wishes that the negro would
shake his hand so he could find out, and to see if the
color rubs off, but the negro turns away and heads for
the bus which will take him back to the city.

Fifth Grade

There are now girls in his class. Two of them. Alice is plain-looking and lives on a farm past the state highway. She is also in his Sunday school class. Judy lives on a farm near the highway bordering the eastern side of town. She is chunky but has a pretty face, dark hair, and dark eyes which echo the smile she always has for him. They like each other, trade cookies and sandwiches at lunch time, and he sympathizes with her whenever the other boys call her stinky.

There is also a new boy for him to play with, a fourth grader who lives at the end of the straight stretch of road beyond Grandma's house. Kenny is the oldest of several boys. His only sister is a year younger.

It is a time of sickness for Jonathan. He loses two weeks of school, throws up once on his desk and once on the playground, and is sent home both times. At night, he often lies in bed moaning for Mother as his body sinks toward an oblivion that refuses to take him. When the doctor comes on a professional visit, Mother hands Jonathan a jar and instructs him to make water.

"What?" he asks, feeling as though some mysterious part of life has passed by without his knowledge.

190

"I said, make water."

"What?"

"Make water," she says, glancing down at the jar.

"In this?" he asks, holding the jar up to her face.

Mother nods then starts to leave the room.

"But, what do you mean?" he wants to know, hoping to avoid a foolish mistake.

"I said, make water," she says again and walks out, leaving him holding the bottle.

Sweating more from uncertainty than illness, he urinates into the jar, then, with fingers crossed, carries it to her.

On winter nights, he helps Sis with her homework, dictating as she practices shorthand or reading her English assignments for general criticism. Once, she writes a story about a large-eyed orphan girl with serious problems, and he is amazed at his sister's talent.

Later, in his bedroom, insomnia keeps him awake. Most nights, he runs the same fantasy through his mind, with only minor changes, in an attempt to fall asleep: He is a cowboy-outlaw, sometimes named Tim, sometimes Jeff, sometimes Biff, a member of a gang which robs banks or stagecoaches, although he—Tim, Jeff, or Biff—always gives his share to the poor and oppressed. In the end, he is ambushed by a well-meaning sheriff, and although Tim, Jeff, or Biff could easily outshoot the lawman, he refuses to do so and takes a bullet in the chest. As he lies dying, people gather around to sympathize and to remark on what a good person he really is— was—and what a shame it is that he is about to die. As blood flows from the wound and he nears his last painful breath, he forgives the sheriff, tells all the crying people that it is all right, then goes limp in everlasting sleep. Sometimes he must play the scene through several times but even that doesn't work.

He continues to paint pictures of the sun going down behind the woods and mountains. At Christmas time, he draws a large picture of the three wise men traveling to Bethlehem on camels and takes it to school where Mrs. Wilson hangs it on the wall above the blackboard. About this time, she proudly announces that there

191

is an artist and there is a writer in the class; James is the artist and Jonathan the writer.

Jonathan is not pleased to hear this. He would prefer to be known as an artist because writing is not the least bit enjoyable. Although stories come easily to mind, the physical work involved in putting the words on paper is so unpleasant as to be a form of torture.

The best part of being a fifth grader is that smaller children now look up to him and come to him with their problems. He rolls up their pant cuffs, ties their shoelaces, buttons their coats, and umpires their ball games. He is delighted to receive their thanks and smiles as payment.

One day, the school sends the students on a bus trip to the state capital. On the way there, on a dare from James, Jonathan kisses the eighth grade girl he is sitting with. The principal, Mr. Cobbs, shakes his head in mild disapproval, but Jonathan believes he has proven something to the older boys and to himself. At the capitol building, he makes a point of walking beside the policeman who is their guide and nearly explodes with happiness when the man accepts a stick of gum from him. At the museum, he and a few eighth grade boys are caught running down the back stairs and are kicked out of the building. All in all, he considers it a very successful day.

On his final report card, he receives an E in every subject but art, for which he is given an S. Arithmetic gets a final mark of 92; English, 97; Silent Reading, 98; Spelling, 97; Penmanship, 86; Language, 98; Health & Safety, 89; Science, 85; Social Studies, 99; Art Handwork, S.

On his Metropolitan Achievement Test, at age 11.3, he receives a score of 57 in Reading, a Grade Equivalent of 7.7, and an Age Equivalent of 13.2; Vocabulary 56, 7.0, 12.7; Average Reading X, 7.4, 12.4; Arithmetic Fundamentals 40, 6.3, 11.10; Average Arithmetic X, 6.2, blank; English 58, 7.8, 13.4; Literature 57, 7.7, 13.2; History and Civics 53, 7.3, 12.10; Geography 48, 6.8, 12.4; Spelling 47, 6.7, 12.3; Total 45.3, 7.0, 12.7.

Joe

Joe enters the room while Jonathan is listening to the Grand Ole Opry. He goes to the radio and turns the dial to a jazz station. He ignores his brother's protests; leans against the woodstove. His eyes become distant and merry as his head bobs to the music and his hands slap out the beat against the grating on top.

Jonathan confronts Joe with clenched fists. Joe ignores him until the song is over, then grins down at the tearful anger. "You're really mad, aren't you?"

"It isn't fair."

"You want to hit me?"

Before the offer can be withdrawn, Jonathan sends his fist upward in roundhouse fashion to clip Joe neatly on the chin, but the only reaction is a cheerful wink.

"Not like that. You'll break your thumb."

It is tucked inside the fingers and Jonathan suddenly realizes how vulnerable that makes it.

"Like this." Joe pulls the thumb out then reshapes the fist properly, "next time, do it that way."

Jonathan stares at the fist for a long time, part of him grateful for the lesson, but he feels he has been taken advantage of. Deep down, the resentment lingers, the bitter thought that the biggest and strongest always win.

Art Appreciation

Frankie and Andy are leaning over James's desk. All three giggle noisily. James catches Jonathan's attention, then nods at their female classmates and toward the book on his desktop. It is obvious that the boys are teasing the girls, trying to annoy and distract them. When Alice glances back over her shoulder to see what is so funny, James points at a picture in his book and Jonathan, caught up in the game, leans over to take a look, giggling as he does.

"Jonathan!" Mrs. Wilson says harshly, glancing up from her desk. "Sit back in your seat."

He obeys, and the room falls silent.

"I want you to stay in during recess."

Jonathan gasps in disbelief, wondering how the other boys have managed to escape punishment, but says nothing.

When recess arrives and the room empties, Mrs. Wilson slides two desks together in front of the room. "Come up here, Jonathan," she says, indicating that he is to take one of the seats. They sit together, and Mrs. Wilson opens the book which had been laying there.

"It wasn't nice to laugh at this picture."

195

He blinks his eyes in disbelief. She is referring to a painting of a naked lady. "That's not what we were looking at," he protests but suddenly wonders if that is true. He had only pretended to see the picture in James's book in order to irritate Alice.

"There's nothing dirty about the human body," Mrs. Wilson continues, as though he hadn't spoken.

"I know it. We weren't... "

"I'm surprised at you, Jonathan. I expect that kind of behavior from the other boys but not from you."

"Yeah, but... "

"God created our bodies in His own likeness. The human body is a beautiful thing. There is nothing dirty or shameful about it."

"I know that. I'm trying to... "

"Listen to me. Don't argue. The human body is like a temple. You shouldn't... "

He lets her continue the lecture without interruption, but his mind wanders and he does not hear much of it. He is thinking how funny this is, how he would like to laugh, and wonders if he should tell the others about Mrs. Wilson's mistake but decides not to.

He is aware of her hand on his shoulder and sincerity in her voice and figures it will hurt her feelings if she believes he hasn't taken her concern seriously. So, when she has finished the talk and asks, "Do you understand what I've told you?", he nods his head and she returns, satisfied, to her desk and he returns to his.

Kenny and Others

  Kenny is a left-hander. With his long, sweeping stroke, he can hit the ball almost as far as Frankie, though not with as much consistency. Even so, he prefers to play ball with seventh and eighth graders rather than boys his own age.

  Nights after school, Jonathan plays with Kenny, his sister, and brothers at their place. Mother does not like Kenny because he is loud and irritating, and she does not encourage his visits to her house.

  Jonathan also has doubts about Kenny. The boy delights in annoying others. He does not let up once he starts, and this habit causes many squabbles which end with each threatening to sue the other for millions of dollars. Just as bad is his farmer's English: He says "axe" for "ask", "follow ball" for "foul ball", "empire" for "umpire", "did-ent" for "didn't", and persistently uses double negatives.

  Even worse is his lack of modesty. He is not embarrassed to wear pants which have a hole in the seat, swim in his underwear at the sand bar, or pee in front of his sister, Lizzie, as they walk home from school with Jonathan. Kenny also delights in bullying her, scornfully mocking her for being a girl, laughing when her dress is up and loudly instructing Jonathan to look at her underwear as she walks away bawling.

Jonathan enjoys the rare moments he is alone with Lizzie more than all the time he spends with Kenny. He likes to play stretch with her because he knows he will win and because she often rubs her crotch upon surrendering in pain. Just as good, to his way of thinking, is that her talk, though polite with innocence, is also uninhibited, like the time she told of one boy kicking another in the privates and the other boy hopping about in agony. He knows that she admires him and likes him for respecting her, and he likes being kind to her.

Their neighbor's little girl is also innocent, but he feels different about her. She is about four, very pretty, and as she swings from a tree branch or climbs onto a picnic table, exposing spotlessly clean and neat underwear and perfectly formed thighs, he feels a longing in his chest that he cannot understand. It is as though his heart is on fire, burning with a desire that has no name or objective, yet is as substantial as the flames. He wants to reach out and touch her sweet face, to make her dark eyes look into his if only for a moment, to bring a smile to her face.

One day, when Kenny and the others go in for supper, the little girl goes with Jonathan to the rear of the house. He has planned this moment for a long time and knows exactly what he has to do.

"Do you wanta wrestle?" he asks playfully.

She nods her head.

It is a cool day and she is wearing a snowsuit, but he does not consider this a problem. He throws his arm around her neck and flips her gently to the ground. For a moment, he lets her grab him in a headlock, then he wrestles her down onto her back. He takes her foot in his hands, braces his foot against her crotch and pulls on the leg. The idea is for her to complain of being hurt, after which he will apologize and ask to look to see if any damage has been done.

"Don't," she says and tries to free herself.

Jonathan lets go then helps her to her feet. "I'm

sorry. Did I hurt you?"

The little girl doesn't reply but walks slowly away toward her house. He watches sadly and with a growing sense of guilt, hoping she will not tell on him. He knows he has lost her as a friend.

He goes to the front of the house to sit on the porch and wait for Kenny, thinking he will have much less happiness to look forward to on future visits, hating himself because it is his own fault.

Laurie

Some boys caught Jonathan talking to Laurie, a sixth grader, on the playground after school. James yelled, "Ooooooooohhh! I know your girlfriend."

"Jonathan loves Laurie," Donald yelled.

"I do not!" Jonathan replied, but they persisted in the accusation. He would not have complained if they had said this about him and Judy, but he felt little affection for this girl.

"Why don't you kiss her?" Kenny said, laughing as though it was funny.

"Shut up!" he shouted, his eyes beginning to moisten.

When the teasing continued, Jonathan ran inside the schoolhouse and up the stairs. By the time he got to the principal's office, tears were streaming down his cheeks. He opened the door and saw the man seated behind his desk.

"Mr. Cobbs," he blurted, "those kids are all saying I love Laurie."

Even though the tears nearly blinded Jonathan, he could see a look of amusement come to Mr. Cobbs's face as he turned it in his direction. The principal calmly said, "Well, don't you?"

Jonathan felt crushed by this failure of authority to perform its duty or to even care about his suffering. "No!" he yelled, then slammed the door shut.

The playground was empty by the time he got back outside, but he found Laurie in front of the store, talking to a classmate. Kenny and a couple of men were sitting on the porch, drinking soda. Joe was walking up the hill, unseen. Jonathan walked over to Laurie and, with lingering tears, shouted into her face, "I don't love you."

"Oh, yes you do," she replied merrily. She grabbed his hands then swung him in circles around her own spinning body, laughing as she did.

The men on the porch leaned back to enjoy the spectacle, as Joe later described it to Mother in derogatory fashion, while Kenny stood idly by.

Jonathan could not pull himself free and knew it would not be honorable to kick or fight her. Frustrated, not knowing what to do, he could only cry harder.

Suddenly, a powerful hand gripped his arm and yanked him violently free of Laurie. He looked up, stunned, into his brother's face.

"Go home!" Joe said angrily and gave him a shove in that direction.

Humiliated, Jonathan obeyed. He walked rapidly away until he was around the bend and out of their sight then slowed his pace.

Kenny caught up with him and apologized for not helping.

"You were making fun of me, too."

"I'm sorry. I didn't mean it."

They finished the walk in silence. Jonathan ignored Kenny's meek, "I'll see you," when they parted.

He entered the house to find Mother preparing supper. He told her what had happened: "Laurie was picking on me in front of everybody, but Joe grabbed me and made me go home."

Mother ignored him, so he went into the living room to suffer alone, grumbling as he left her, "It isn't fair."

Toward a Final Sunset

Jonathan and Frankie are rolling down the hill across from the school, one boy on top and then the other. It is roll--pause--roll--pause--roll--pause nearly to the fence at the bottom. Neither boy can get the advantage on the other. There is a grunt, Jonathan rolls over and comes atop Frankie, holds him for one breath, then Frankie grunts, rolls and comes out atop Jonathan.

At the top of the hill, where all three had been only moments ago, James sits with his chin resting on his knees, a look of perplexity on his face, as though he has forgotten who to root for.

Finally, Jonathan stretches his arms out from his sides so he can roll no farther. He takes a deep breath, then says, "What are we fighting about, anyway?"

Frankie says nothing but stares blankly back at him. The bully, too, has forgotten what started the fight. He gets up off Jonathan and, together, they climb the hill toward James.

Jonathan wonders if the climb is worth the effort. He knows he will soon come tumbling down again; if not this hill then another. Life, he is convinced, is all down-hill. The people on top are always there to push him

202

back, and unless he fights he will never make it to the top. But he vows that he will never fight again, no matter who the bully or what the provocation, and no matter what he stands to lose. He convinces himself that fighting is morally wrong, that its main purpose is to hurt an opponent and to make oneself look superior in the eyes of others. He is content to let someone else be first at bat or in line, to be the captain of a team or leader of a venture, to be smarter or stronger if that is important to them, to be number one in a world where all are contenders but himself.

If only the bullies would stop picking on him, he thinks. If only they would leave him alone and stop trying to force him to live his life under their rules. If only Joe could see their wickedness sometime, could catch them performing their evil acts and come to his rescue, but he knows that Joe would more than likely take their side.

If only Father would stop picking on him about his nervous habits; if only he could stop wetting in bed; if only the terrifying spells of sleeptime paralysis and inability to breath would cease; if only he could learn that terrible secret of girlhood, he would begin to feel human.

At night, he lies in bed listening to Mother and Father talking downstairs, their voices so low he cannot make out the words. He wants them to be talking about him but knows they are not. He wants to be with them but knows they do not want him.

His throat becomes hot and tight and he silently cries. He gazes through the window at the dark sky and thinks of running away, but there is no place to go. He wants to take his own life so everyone will know how much he has suffered and how cruel they have been to him, but, as he imagines his hand pushing a knife into his chest, the burning and pain are too much to bear and he has to withdraw it. Yet, there is no other way; when he speaks, no one listens, and when he cries, they turn their backs to him with revulsion.

He sometimes wonders if Mother and Father are his real parents, or if, perhaps, they had found him, as a baby, somewhere in the woods and had reluctantly brought him home, the way Superman's parents had done, and if that is their reason for hating him.

Voices from other rooms seem to come from other worlds, as though he is really dead after all and is only a spirit unable to communicate with the living. An uncontrollable grief circulates among his fears, leaves him shivering as though he was cold. He sinks into the bed, deeper and deeper, floating down into the night as sleep rises slowly to meet him.

And, when the snow comes, he knows there will be no more summers. Through the door window, he sees long, slender shadows reaching out for him like death's fingers. He sees the future darkening into one final sunset, the red ball burning through the webbed trees of his mind, going darker and darker until all that remains is the grave. He feels the bitter cold of an eternal winter seeping through the cracks of the door, reaching in with icy hands to crush his mind.

He wonders what will come to destroy him, the outer world of indifference or the unsatisfied hunger for knowledge and caring that spreads through him like cancer.

He doesn't care how he dies, as long as oblivion comes swiftly. If the pen was really mightier than the sword, he would write himself to death.

"Dear God," he prays, "please let me die so they'll all feel sorry for me."

And a tear trickles onto his pillow.

Epilogue 8

The world is still dark but Little Boy has come to a new level of awareness. He tries to return to his old world in order to set things right, but certain forces block his way and blow him on waves of consciousness farther and farther away, until there is no chance that he will ever find the path back to his brick house and the mysteries which lie beyond it. Even his sense of sadness has been torn from him and he watches images float by with a coldness he doesn't feel. He catches a fleeting glimpse of a dark-haired girl, her eyes touching a secret part of him. Then there is Simon, patting the severed head of a dead man, a head blackened by the sun and by decay, eye sockets gaping with the white of maggots, cracked lips formed into a death grimace, smelling of the grave and worms. Little Boy wonders how Simon could ever have loved such a horrid thing.